FIRST PEDIGREE MURDER

MELISSA CLEARY

BERKLEY PRIME CRIME, NEW YORK

This book is a Berkley Prime Crime original edition, and has never been previously published.

FIRST PEDIGREE MURDER

A Berkley Prime Crime Book / published by arrangement with the author

PRINTING HISTORY
Berkley Prime Crime edition / July 1994

ISBN: 0-425-14299-X

Berkley Prime Crime Books are published by
The Berkley Publishing Group,
200 Madison Avenue, New York, NY 10016.
The name BERKLEY PRIME CRIME and the BERKLEY PRIME CRIME
design are trademarks of Berkley Publishing Corporation.

PRINTED IN THE UNITED STATES OF AMERICA

10 9 8 7 6 5 4 3 2 1

MORE MYSTERIES FROM THE
BERKLEY PUBLISHING GROUP . . .

For D.

FIRST PEDIGREE MURDER

PROLOGUE

"Your money or your life."

This was the feed line. Some say only a minute went by. Others put in claims for a minute thirty . . . two minutes . . . even two and a half minutes, before the stickup man, played by Mel Blanc, followed up with his loud "Well?"

And Jack Benny responded, "I'm thin-king."

It was the longest, loudest laugh in the history of radio.

Benny's great rival in those days was Fred Allen, of course. His great line was, "You can stash all the genuine sentiment in Hollywood in a flea's navel and still have room for two caraway seeds and a producer's heart."

Jack Benny and Mel Blanc are gone now. So too for many years is Fred Allen. Gone with them are Kate Smith, Major Bowes, and Fibber McGee and Molly. Whether these individuals and their brethren were geniuses or just time-wasters like all the rest is a matter of some debate, I suppose.

All you have to remember is—radio was an art form once.

While most of the great performers from those days are gone, their fans, at least some of them, are still going strong. At the same time that many of their generation went placidly, yea willingly, to television, a goodly number stuck with their radios. They remain radio fanatics to this day, listening to what little new radio drama, comedy, or musical variety programs are being produced, or, more commonly, to rebroadcasts of the Golden Age material coming to them from on-air Hall of Fame curators such as Max Schmeed.

One fan, a resident of the bustling Midwest town of Palmer (home of amateur sleuth Jackie Walsh and her canny canine assistant, Jake), regularly recorded these rebroadcasts. This fan's favorite program was *I Love a Mystery*. The attraction of this particular program was that many of the episodes depicted simple, foolproof methods of committing the perfect murder.

It just goes to show you that simple entertainments can be educational as well.

CHAPTER 1

The new Radio Arts Building certainly looked like a great place to loaf and chase cats. A large gray building, it had many cool, dark alcoves; a good number of sturdy, surrounding trees; and a series of access ramps that a fella could make good time down if a cat or squirrel were to come along, suddenlike.

Having let her dog, Jake, get his view of the building, Jackie Walsh feasted her own eyes on the structure.

"What a beauty," she said softly. The glittering green and silver six-story structure had meant a lot of work for the grateful Palmer construction crews. The remaining metal workers in the area had really knocked themselves out over this building, determined to show their old employers the good work they could still do if only given a chance.

The Radio Arts Building's conning tower, once an embarrassing eyesore, had been given a twin and now together they stretched like the arms of Colossus beckoning the gods.

The gods did not come, however. Mere millionaires presented themselves instead. As Jackie and Jake stood admiring the building outside, a meeting proceeded inside. Included were Stuart Goodwillie, Palmer's great crank and bottled water millionaire; his older brother, the great industrial chemist, Mannheim Goodwillie; and the shambling head of the Rodgers University radio program,

Keith Monahan (not a millionaire).

"Are you as proud of the new Josiah Goodwillie Radio Facility as I am?" Keith Monahan demanded, gently putting his hand on Stuart Goodwillie's shoulder.

The bantam cock industrialist looked witheringly at Monahan's offending appendage until the mortified radio instructor removed it.

"Don't touch me again for any reason whatever," Goodwillie instructed.

"Yes, sir. Sorry."

"As to your question about whether or not I am proud of this building named after my father—a man who would spin in his grave like the blades of an eggbeater if he had any idea of the cost of this glittering mausoleum—my answer is, I can't stand the thought of the place." Goodwillie tried to spit on the plush maroon wall-to-wall carpeted floor, but found that his throat was too dry.

"Would you like something to drink, sir?" Monahan asked quickly.

"No, no," Goodwillie responded with patently fake kindly cheer. "Just leave me to wheeze myself into oblivion. My lawyers will amuse themselves after my passing reducing your university to bankrupt heaps of firewood."

"One minute, sir," Monahan promised, matching an insincere smile of his own to the millionaire's. "I'll get something for you right away." He stepped to one of the wall intercoms and then turned his head back to Mannheim Goodwillie. "How about you, sir? A drink, anything?"

The older Goodwillie, seated on a straight-backed chair, turned his warm countenance to Monahan. "No. Thank you very much, young man."

Monahan depressed the talk lever on the intercom. "Spike, try to find Sylvie or Tim, will you? Tell them I said to bring some drinks up for our guests in the green room, right away." As Monahan signed off, ignoring the grumblings of the ancient stagehand on the other end, he turned back to hear Mannheim Goodwillie admonish his brother.

"Really, Stuart, there is no excuse for your treatment of this poor young man . . ."

Goodwillie regarded Monahan with what at best could be called withering scorn. "If he's old enough to run a radio station, he's old enough to take his medicine like a good little soldier, isn't that right, er . . . ?"

"Keith, sir. Keith Monahan."

"Carnero." Stuart Goodwillie turned to his bodyguard, a massive South American with a formidable walking cast on his left leg who bore a startling resemblance to the young Boris Karloff. "If this fellow tries to interrupt or impose his name on me again, squeeze his throat until his eyeballs bulge."

"Stuart . . . really."

"Shut up, Mannheim," Stuart Goodwillie barked. He then turned a glittering hawk's eye on the Radio Arts instructor. "We were speaking of something important. What was it?"

"You were denigrating my life's dream, sir," Monahan reminded the millionaire.

"That's right," Goodwillie cackled. "Young fellow, I'm going to explain something to you and hope to Hades you haven't been educated beyond the intelligence needed to understand me. I gave the money to the building fund for your albatross radio station under duress. Six months ago your intrepid colleague, Ms. Walsh, and her idiot policeman friend, er . . . ?"

"Lieutenant McGowan, sir," Monahan provided. He then stopped short, realizing that he had violated Goodwillie's prohibition against interrupting.

"Pop his eyes like cherrystones, Carnero!" Goodwillie ordered.

Carnero immediately took a step toward the over-weight radio instructor.

All of a sudden young Sylvie Thompson, a student in Radio Arts just coming radiantly into bloom, stepped into the room with a tray of tall glasses of ice cube-laden liquid. "Excuse me, Keith? You wanted drinks?"

"Ah!" Goodwillie bleated, immediately donning the role of kindly old uncle. "Saved by the belle! Come in, young lady. How nice of you to trouble yourself for two filthy rich elderly bachelor gentlemen."

Monahan immediately grabbed a glass and a napkin off the tray and brought it over to where Stuart Goodwillie was standing. "Here you are, Mr. Goodwillie." Then turning to the millionaire's seated older brother, he asked, "Are you quite sure you won't join us, sir?"

Mannheim Goodwillie again favored Monahan with his warm smile. "I'm fine, son. Really."

"Yes, so anyway, Keith," Stuart Goodwillie said, draping his arm casually around Monahan's shoulders, as if resuming a conversation. "I'm flattered at the idea of you doing that series of special programs on my life, but what have I done, really, that would be of any interest to anyone? Unless, of course, you count building a massive fortune and a half-dozen fabulous residences here in Palmer and in various pleasure spots throughout the world . . ." Ignoring the chopfallen expression on Monahan's face, Goodwillie concentrated instead on impressing angelic Sylvie Thompson.

Before Goodwillie could go any further, however, Jackie entered the green room, practically at a dead run. "Keith! You're still here. Thank goodness! I had the most awful time getting Peter to meet me outside and take care of Jake. How are you? Don't worry, I have the script with me." The flushed, dark-haired film instructor then caught her breath and took in the surprised looks from the room's other occupants.

Monahan, just happy to see a friendly face, put his

arm around her and announced to the room, "I'd like to introduce, to those of you who don't know her, the lovely Ms. Jacqueline Walsh. Jackie teaches here at the college; she wrote teleplays for a dozen or so of the finest examples of episodic drama in the last twenty years, and as Mr. Goodwillie indicated earlier, she's also Palmer's amateur secret weapon against crime."

"Man," Jackie responded. "I like that introduction a lot. Did you by chance happen to get that on tape?"

"I don't know." Monahan crossed to the wall intercom. "Spike! You taping us down here?"

"Yes, sir, Mr. Monahan. Just as you said, sir."

Monahan turned with a smile, "Voilà."

"I'll take a dozen copies then," Jackie said facetiously. "Send them to all my friends."

"I'm sure we can work that out," Monahan replied smoothly. "Anyway, you were making a point, I believe, Mr. Goodwillie, before we were interrupted?"

"Oh, no," Goodwillie protested meekly. "Just aimlessly prattling, you know, the way old folks do."

"Well," Jackie smiled. "If I may just freshen up?"

"Absolutely," Monahan smiled. "The glorious new Josiah Goodwillie Radio Facility's 'Princess Suite' is, I believe, right over there."

Sylvie then stood back up with her tray and unclaimed glass. "Uh, is it okay if I go now, Keith? I mean, if you have what you need?"

"Of course, Sylvie," Monahan smiled charmingly. "Thanks a lot for bringing these up."

Stuart Goodwillie, watching Sylvie leave the room, mumbled, "Yes, yes. Lovely ladies. Fine fresh flowers of Palmer's youth. Brings an old man to tears . . ."

The moment the ladies were out of earshot, however, Goodwillie turned to Monahan and resumed his tirade. "I was caught brown-handed, do you understand me, Monahan? That meddling woman who just came in caught me trying to dump four hundred pounds of ungodly East Indian spice in the reservoir to improve my bottled water sales. In return for not being prosecuted to the fullest extent of the law, I had to make a pact with the devil to pour my hard-earned, sweat-stained dollars into a temple for a communications medium that was dead as far back as my father's time. That's why I insisted you call this place the Josiah Goodwillie Radio Facility, so that you would invoke that outraged good man's angry ghost to haunt these callow halls!"

Then, as if possessing a sixth sense, Stuart Goodwillie turned to greet Jackie's reappearance. "Ah, Ms. Walsh. Lovely, lovely. What was it Romeo said about Juliet, 'Arise fair sun' and so on . . ."

Jackie blushed and turned to Monahan. "Oh, you're still talking. I hate to interrupt. Can I meet you in your office?"

"Sure. Here. You'll need this to get in." Monahan unclipped his magnetic strip pass identifier badge and put it in Jackie's hand. "Take a seat in my office. Help yourself from the fridge. I just have to get a couple of publicity pictures taken with our great benefactors here and I'll be right down."

"Okay." Jackie smiled at both Monahan and Goodwillie in turn before exiting the room.

"Such a lovely, capable . . . trim turn of the ankle does it every time," Goodwillie mumbled, waiting for Jackie to pass out of earshot. He then wheeled to resume his attack on Monahan. "Suffice to say then, I resent every cent I've poured down this charity toilet from the very start, and would cheerfully cut your throat from ear to ear for a shiny dime."

"Really, Stuart," Mannheim protested, "is it necessary to go through this every time you are tricked into donating money to a worthy cause?"

"When I give pennies, perhaps not!" Stuart Goodwillie responded loudly. "But when I give millions of dollars to fund a radio station, an entirely frivolous luxury in the midst of a depression when most people are too tired to do anything but eat, sleep, and work—I think my largesse gives me a right to complain if I so choose. Wouldn't you say, lad?"

Monahan nodded dumbly.

"I'm so glad," Goodwillie sneered. Adoring profiles of Stuart Goodwillie in various business-oriented publications seldom mentioned the fact that he really wasn't a very nice man.

"I granted this white elephant two million of my hard-earned bottled water dollars," Goodwillie continued, his eyes glittering with malevolent light. "When the costs on this building had reached nearly *three* million, I turned off the money spring. Call me an old crab, but I thought it high time to stop paying several hundred horny-handed fumblers and incompetents to snore on their shovels while all the time collecting triple union overtime. My brother Mannheim here was kind enough to take over the funding with money from his own foundation. Now you gesture like some demented pointer at the walls of a bog of financial quicksand; a building that ran almost one and a half million dollars over budget, and expect me to cry a grateful little tear. If I were anything like my father, I'd have a few truck drivers stuff you in an old trunk and dump you in the deepest depths of the Palmer reservoir . . ."

Goodwillie turned again at the instant Sylvie Thompson returned, sticking in a golden blond head that had been freshly combed to ask, "How are the drinks, gentlemen? All right?"

Holding up his untouched glass, Goodwillie prepared to sip from it and simpered, "Wonderful, wonderful. A veritable Jove's ambrosia."

"Great. Well, excuse me." Sylvie exited and Stuart Goodwillie spit out the contents of his mouth on an expensive leather couch.

"What sort of pigswill are you serving me?!"

Monahan was taken aback. "Er, I believe that's ginger ale, sir. A very reputable Canadian company makes it and . . ."

Stuart Goodwillie turned crossly to Carnero. "What's the matter with you, man? Are you a victim of sleeping sickness? Go out to my limousine and bring in my flask. Could you possibly be less competent? I hired you to protect my life, not daydream while I writhe before you in spasms of dehydration. Your brother, Julio, God bless his memory, would have flipped a stiletto through this man's heart at the first breath of blasphemy."

As Carnero exited the room, Stuart Goodwillie turned back to Monahan. "Now listen to me, blubber boy. I agreed to submit to a *brief* photograph session. My brother agreed to stoop to a *brief* radio interview for your adoring dozens, but all we've done so far is listen to you babble like an idiot while your staff tries to do me in with a death potion of sugared sewer water. Let's get cracking, Monahan. You may be in academia, but I have a life to lead."

"Yes, I quite understand," Monahan replied. "I hate to keep inconveniencing you, Mr. Goodwillie, as I apparently continue doing."

"Well, if it's all that apparent," Goodwillie rasped, "why don't you stop?"

"I'll certainly try, sir," Monahan promised. "The KCIN feature team are on their way, sir . . ."

"When did you call them?" Goodwillie demanded. "Five minutes ago? Do you ever do anything right? Is it true your students have to come in at regular intervals to massage your heart and lungs so you don't topple over backward from sheer inertia?"

"I'm very sorry," the normally cheerful radio instructor forced out. "Apparently, Ms. Jacobs had a flat tire on the way over and . . ."

"Marcella Jacobs?!" Goodwillie ranted. "What sort

of bilge are you shoveling? The woman's a newspaper reporter, you ninny!"

"Well, no, sir," Monahan explained. "She was demoted to the newspaper's television station, sir—remember—at your insistence, as a price for calling off that multimillion-dollar lawsuit you filed . . ."

"Oh, yes, yes. Whatever." Goodwillie waved his hand negligently. "I leave the memorizing of such dreary facts to my clerks. That's what they're there for. So, how do you intend to amuse us while we waste our remaining declining years cooling our heels here in your basement rec room?"

"Well," Monahan responded, thinking quickly, "I could set up an old radio tape for you in the VIP listening room. Anything you want to hear. We have an extensive library."

Stuart Goodwillie made a face and waved toward his dozing brother. "Thank you, Monahan, for your spectacular generosity, but perhaps you can come up with a suggestion at least appealing enough to keep my brother awake."

"Well, how about this?" Monahan improvised. "Why don't we go down and record your brother's interview now? And you can watch and see how we work and how your brother acquits himself on radio?"

"What part of the word 'no' didn't you understand, you imbecile!" Stuart Goodwillie raged. "I am not interested in radio. I hate it with a bright white smoldering passion. I said *amusement*! Why don't you offer to throw us to the floor and beat us with steel rods?" With that, Stuart Goodwillie turned to see his returning bodyguard. "Oh, here you are, Carnero. Enjoyed your nap, we hope? Perhaps next time I send you on a life and death errand you can amble down to the local video store and rent a movie."

"Excuse me, sir," interrupted the long-suffering retainer. "The reporter and her film crew are here."

"Oh," Stuart Goodwillie cried out. "Pass me confetti so I can dance a simple peasant jig of joy."

The tall, once redheaded, now gray-blond, husky-voiced reporter rushed into the room. "Hello . . . Sorry we're late. Oh, boy. Right? Anyway, Mr. Monahan . . . Mr., uh, Goodwillie . . . Mr., er, uh, another Goodwillie. I'm Marcella Jacobs. I'm going to make you rich and famous. Not that you aren't already."

"Stop your twittering!" Goodwillie barked. "I'll have your head in a hatbox if you keep me waiting again. *Of course*, we're doing this because there's a possibility that a sympathetic portrait of my brother and myself may sell a few more bottles of Goodwillie Good Water to the great unwashed public."

Carnero handed Goodwillie a silver cup of liquid poured from his special flask. The industrialist took the cup without acknowledgment.

"If those Johnny-morons," Goodwillie resumed, "are stupid enough to think that there's any correlation between a good bottle of water and a good heart, then I guess it's up to me to help them cling to their cherished illusions." Goodwillie then reached a bony hand to shake his dozing older brother's shoulder.

"Wake up, Mannheim. Torquemada and her boys are here. Where are we to be force-marched now? I wonder. Out into some stuffy hall to bake our brains under banks of insufferably bright lights?"

"No, no, not at all, Mr. Goodwillie," Marcella replied, grimly summoning up a smile. "We can go anywhere you find comfortable."

"Ah, then we'll be *speeding* toward my mansion."

"Well, no."

Stuart Goodwillie then turned abruptly to his brother. "Mannheim, do me a favor, will you, old chap? Descend to the torture dungeon and hurry through your interview. I will submit to the humiliations concocted by this pitiful crew of bumblers and then we shall go home and mourn our departed florins."

Mannheim nodded and, leaning heavily on his cane, pulled himself to his feet. "Mr. Monahan, I am at your service."

CHAPTER 2

As Jackie poured herself a glass of the bottled water distributed by Goodwillie's great competitor, McKean Pharmaceuticals, she admired the pictures on the wall of Keith Monahan's new office. There were hundreds of glossies; some featured Monahan posing with celebrities—everyone from an elderly Harold "Great Gildersleeve" Peary to the brilliant writers Oriana and Bill D'Andrea.

There were autographed pictures, probably worth many hundreds of dollars to collectors, of many of the greats of radio—Jack Webb, Arch Kobler, John Barrymore, Ken Murray, and Minnie Pearl.

All very impressive, Jackie thought to herself.

She was waiting to discuss a radio version of one of her unproduced screenplays with the radio instructor. It was a script that Jackie could see would adapt nicely to radio and she was tempted to authorize it on one condition—that the leading role had to be played by Ronald Dunn, the handsome veteran actor who she had met recently on an unexpected trip to Los Angeles.

While Jackie waited upstairs, Keith Monahan talked to his student engineer Tim Falk. Falk was a thin, high-strung youth with dark-framed glasses who had recently discarded the Lawrence of Arabia headdress he had favored in the old, overheated, college-barn Radio Arts Building for a baseball cap. This cap, incidentally, despite great pressure from his fellow students, Tim insisted on wearing correctly, bill forward.

"Tim," Monahan all but whispered in the student's ear. "Our first guest, Mr. Mannheim Goodwillie, is like Zeus, VIP God of VIP Gods. Do you follow me? Whatever we have to do—roll on a moment's notice, cut tape, fill with musical cues, give the guy a gee-whiz footrub if he wants one—let's do it, all right? Believe me, whatever token humiliation you may feel will be a mote in an elephant's eye compared to the hand kissing I've done these last six months."

Tim nodded his understanding and Keith straightened his six-foot, large-boned frame, currently holding on it some two hundred eighty pounds of fat and muscle, and looked down at the bullring where the other guests scheduled for today's gala program sat waiting.

First up, there was Her Honor, Jane Bellamy, the mayor of Palmer, an elderly, chain-smoking, much surgically sculpted dragoness with jalapeño-colored hair, dark, widespread eyes, and large lips positively swollen with lipstick.

Mayor Bellamy would be explaining to the public why this still was not a good time to reveal the public works Stuart Goodwillie had promised the Palmer public after a decade of tainting the town's water supply.

Next to the mayor was Cosmo Gordon, the outdoorsy Palmer medical examiner—originally a Canadian, it was said. It was also said that Dr. Gordon was not above sneaking an occasional shot of rye when he was not, strictly speaking, on duty.

On this occasion the medical examiner looked remarkably sober. Monahan knew this was undoubtedly due to Dr. Gordon's choice of subject matter. Gordon was speaking on the program on behalf of a committee he chaired to raise money to erect a statue in Palmer Park to Matthew Dugan, a brave undercover hero cop who had died in the line of duty due to job-related stress,

alcoholism, and poor nutrition—though some people in
Palmer still whispered rumors about other, more scandalous circumstances surrounding his death. Monahan
had heard from someone earlier that Dugan's widow
and children were now living in the same duplex on
Isabella Lane as Jackie Walsh.

Next to Cosmo Gordon was Henry Obermaier, the
president of Rodgers University, who had recently ten-
dered his resignation to accept a job at a prestigious New
England university.

A good mix, Monahan thought. He wished he could
have gotten that woman associated with the Free Merida
Green movement. The president of the organization, a
Ms. Blue, had said she would try to just show up, but
that she had some sort of schedule conflict.

Seeing that all was relatively well, Keith nodded to
Spike Fitzgerald, the elderly stagehand the Palmer Stage-
hands Union had made them hire as an engineer.

The Local 72 man nodded in his turn to Ral Perrin, the
young cinematography TA who was filming the whole
event for Fred Jackson's documentary class.

"Ready to roll tape," Monahan spoke into the headset.
He then sat down at his seat on the small stage. "Sylvie!
You can bring out Mr. Goodwillie now if he's ready.
Okay? Thirty seconds. Here we go. Music out and—"

"Hello, FM fans, this is Keith Monahan here talking to
you from KRJD, the independent radio station operating
out of Rodgers University right here in beautiful Palmer,
Ohio. Well, as they used to say in my father's day, 'Put
down your pet bird,' we've got a heckuva program
for you today. Mayor Bellamy is with us. Dr. Cosmo
Gordon, the medical examiner, is here and . . ."

Cuing Tim to prepare a cut to music, Monahan paused
in midsentence as he saw a forcible, big-sweatshirt-and-
pants-garbed, fierce female figure push her way past
Walter Hupfelt, the Palmer security chief, and dash
toward the bullpen.

"Yes, and, uh, Alice Blue of the Free Merida Green movement has been kind enough to stop by," Monahan ad-libbed quickly. "And last but not least, our own beloved president is here. I'm not referring to that funny-looking guy in Washington—I mean the outgoing president of Rodgers University, Henry Obermaier."

Henry Obermaier, sweating and uncomfortable in a seldom-worn tuxedo, smiled vacantly.

"Before I get to our special celebrity lineup," Monahan continued, "I want to visit with a very special guest without whom this studio, this program, this very radio station, would not be here to entertain you. I refer, of course, to Mr. Mannheim Goodwillie. Welcome to the program, Mr. Goodwillie."

The ancient chemist sat heavily in the guest chair and then spoke comfortably into the microphone.

"I'm happy . . ."

"Lower the boom," Spike the engineer instructed from up above them as they talked.

"Is that better?" Mannheim asked. "Anyway, I'm very happy to be here."

"And we're delighted to have you," Monahan smiled. "Mr. Goodwillie, you were for many years in charge of the laboratories at Falk & Goodwillie Pharmaceuticals?"

"That's correct," Mannheim responded, answering each question in his slow, warm, precise voice. "I rose to the position of director of laboratories when my father was still head of the company. Mr. Falk was dead by this time. He hurled himself from a building in 1929.

"I maintained my position of director of laboratories during my own tenure as president. Then, when I came back from fighting the war, I resumed my old position under my brother's stewardship of the company. Incidentally, my son Arthur, who recently passed away in an automobile accident, had served as president in the North Africa office of our international pharmaceutical concern and was also the director of laboratories during his administration. His loss is a terrible blow."

"I'm very sorry, Mr. Goodwillie," Monahan responded sympathetically.

"Well, what can you do?" Mannheim sighed. "My family has been very fortunate overall. To each of us must come some tragedy."

"Who will run your pharmaceutical company now?" Monahan asked. "Another of the younger Goodwillie generation?"

"No." Mannheim smiled sadly. "There is no such animal. I had only one child in my marriage. My brother is a bachelor. We are considering selling the pharmaceutical corporation. My brother has his bottled water company now. I am happy in my retirement."

"Well, you're not totally inactive in your retirement, sir," Monahan protested.

"No. Why not?" Mannheim chuckled. "You should see me. Days on end—I sit like a lump."

"But on other days," Monahan blithely launched into his tribute. "You do good works, Mr. Goodwillie. You have given a special chair to the Science department at another university . . ."

"*Assissi of Palmer!*" Mannheim said loudly.

Monahan winced at the mention of Rodgers's fiercest academic competitor and then moved on. "You've given money to the Marx-Wheeler Hospital for a special treatment unit . . ."

Mannheim nodded. "Gout is a terrible thing."

"Yes, I'm sure it is," Monahan said quickly, "and last but not least, you and your brother Stuart donated the money that it took to build this entire building, this entire building named after your father Josiah Goodwillie."

"Yes, that's right," Mannheim confirmed slowly. "And I'll tell you why we did it, Keith. It all starts with a young immigrant boy's finding a peanut still in its shell . . ."

Mannheim Goodwillie had no sooner started into his favorite yarn when all of a sudden he clutched spasmodically at his chest and pitched forward onto the floor by Keith Monahan's feet.

Goodwillie then unfortunately rolled backward on the button that lit up the APPLAUSE sign and the other guests, crew, and small invited audience, not knowing any better, did.

Monahan knew at once it was bad. He stood up and yelled, "Spike! Break tape! Excuse me, everyone! Is there a doctor in the house?"

Cosmo Gordon rushed to the stage where the elderly industrialist lay sprawled and lifeless. He checked the man's pulse, noted the fixed pupils, then reached into the man's shirt. Withdrawing his hand a moment later with a curse, Gordon stuck his fingers into his mouth to cool them.

"Is he sick, Doctor?" Monahan asked at once.

"It's worse than that," Gordon responded, removing his fingers from his mouth. "He's dead, Monahan."

CHAPTER 3

Mannheim Goodwillie was rich enough to be accustomed to being driven about. The ride from Rodgers University to the Palmer office of the medical examiner was provided by the city. It was the last ride intact that Mannheim Goodwillie would ever take.

As Cosmo Gordon, now changed into his work clothes (which consisted of a white shirt, dark tie, the pants and vest to one of a number of elderly gray suits, and a white lab coat), walked through the basement parking lot, he winced at the noise. The outside doors to the river were being closed and their squeaky hinges could be heard all over the building. Somewhere in the body lockers, somebody was opening and shutting drawers. Noises from the laundry indicated that another large mass of linens were being laundered free of any trace of humans.

It unnerved Cosmo.

The medical examiner's office was a source of constant disappointment to him. He had always thought, when he had left his practice as an emergency room doctor in a small Canadian hospital to become an assistant coroner in Palmer, that after years of dealing with a cacophony of human suffering, at least here, working with the dead, it would be quiet.

As he reached the third floor, Cosmo thought sadly of the deceased Mannheim Goodwillie. Ten years ago he would have insisted on doing such a VIP case himself. Now, ever since the death of his friend, Matthew Dugan, Cosmo Gordon left the chore of performing postmortem examinations to other hands.

As he stepped into the autopsy suite, Cosmo saw the other hands in question, his two assistant coroners— Roy Thomas, a youngish, dark-haired energetic boy with a puppy-dog face, and Lee Humphries, the ambitious former medical examiner from Duluth, Minnesota, who made no secret of her designs on his job—demonstrating an organ cutting for a couple of young pathology residents.

At times Cosmo thought, *Well, fair enough, I certainly had designs on old Crook's place when I first started working here.* Today such thoughts irritated him. Then, seeing the two assistant coroners giggling as if they had found something funny, Gordon barked out, "Rule two, doctors! If you can't follow rule two, please leave the premises."

Rule two, Cosmo heard Roy explain to the two young pathology residents, had to do with decorum. You owed the corpse certain dignities. While performing an autopsy you worked quietly and with compassion. You covered the corpse's face with a piece of material, white if possible, before starting the post. You did not laugh, joke, sing, eat, or otherwise crack wise during the entire proceedings. The recently dead still had a few rights in the eyes of the law. No matter who it was.

Cosmo made his way to the back of the autopsy suite and unlocked the door of his own small office. He turned on the light, looked suspiciously at the three potted cacti, which Cosmo had always suspected huddled together and communicated in some way when he was out of the office, then checked the maildrop built into his door for brown folders.

There were three.

Cosmo leafed through the folders quickly and came up with the one he was looking for. Flipping through it, Cosmo Gordon checked through the findings of the Preliminary Postmortem Analysis and read again the surprises—facts he had been apprised of earlier. He then poured himself a thimbleful of rye from a decanter and picked up the phone.

How fair was this, that a good man, who had retired early to devote himself to public works, was dead of a freak accident, while his brother Stuart, a man endlessly devoted to making a buck and chasing, like some elderly balding Harpo Marx, every attractive woman who came across his path, was still alive?

"Hello, put me through to Lieutenant McGowan, please. This is the medical examiner."

A moment later the pleasant, reassuring baritone of his friend Lieutenant Michael McGowan of Homicide was heard on the line. "Hello, Cosmo. What did you *dig* up for me?"

"Spare me this once, Michael," Gordon pleaded. "I have the preliminary on Mr. Goodwillie you wanted so badly."

"Good," McGowan answered, relieved. "You have no idea what kind of pressure Hero Healy is putting on us down here to get this case solved and solved fast. What can you tell me?"

Gordon flipped through the five pages again and finally responded, "This is going to be rather complicated. It would perhaps be easier if we could meet . . ."

"Sure, the Juniper Tavern for a burger and brew?"

"Under the circumstances, Michael," Cosmo's dry voice responded, "the last thing I want to eat right now is cooked meat."

The University Precinct of the Palmer police department was, relatively speaking, a laid-back kind of place. Detectives could usually finish their calls without having constantly to interrupt and put people on hold.

Michael McGowan had a small office near the rest rooms in the back left corner of the precinct's second story.

McGowan had decorated the office simply. The only thing out of the ordinary besides a battered wooden desk, three chairs, and a file cabinet that couldn't lock was a framed copy of a TV-tie-in paperback book from the *Dragnet* series starring Jack Webb.

The lieutenant had often wished for a partner like the ones Joe Friday used to have. Some of the greatest character actors in radio history had stood beside Jack Webb over the years, reading their lines off cue cards, the way he insisted. And these sidekicks had always gotten the best lines, because their boss had an idea that the better the people he hired looked, the better he looked.

In real life detectives seldom work with partners, let alone the same partner. Real detectives do most of their work alone unless they're breaking in someone. On the rare occasions when McGowan did need a partner, he usually requested Detective Sergeant Felix Cruz, a gaunt, pinch-faced Dominican with a nervous habit of rubbing a small, textured piece of mahogany he kept in his coat pocket. It was this detective that McGowan beckoned to as he got off the phone with Cosmo Gordon. "Felix!"

The quietly industrious young sergeant came over at once. "Yes, Lieutenant?"

"I'm going over to see Cosmo Gordon," McGowan explained, getting up from his chair. "He has the autopsy on Mannheim Goodwillie and I guess it's too difficult to go over on the phone."

Cruz nodded. "So you'll be at the Juniper?"

McGowan gave Cruz a look like this was a scandalous suggestion. "I'll be at the ME's, Cruz. Where else would I be going to transact official Homicide Bureau business?"

• • •

In the end, Cosmo and McGowan had Palmer-style chili, sent up from Fred Lear's Sports Bar.

As the doctor fiddled with the temperamental copying machine, McGowan held up his plate of spaghetti mixed in with chili and exclaimed, "Great chili, Cosmo."

Gordon nodded that he agreed. "For a man who plays baseball for a living, he doesn't cook half bad. Anyway, take a look here."

McGowan moved the plate he was holding slightly to one side so he could look down into the flat, oblong Zenker's container holding the late Mannheim Goodwillie's heart.

"See how big the heart is?" the ME pointed with his fork. "Do you know what that means?"

McGowan shrugged. He hated looking at hearts. First of all, they were always brown or, worse, gray-green instead of red like he'd always thought they'd be. Second of all, the heart was shaped nothing like a heart. In fact, most hearts McGowan had seen in his lifetime reminded him of the cow udders he vaguely remembered from his grandfather's Wisconsin ranch.

"Michael . . . ?"

And why, McGowan wondered, did they always leave the coronary arteries intact so that whenever you moved the jar they'd float around like the tendrils of an angry jellyfish?

"Michael!" Gordon raged impatiently. "Do you know what hyperplasia of the heart indicates?"

"Unh, unh," McGowan admitted, taking another forkful of chili and spaghetti. "That he was a super nice guy?"

Cosmo gave the lieutenant a look. "Circulatory problems, my friend. Like a policeman whose diet consists principally of donuts, chili, and coffee, Goodwillie had clogged arteries. Therefore, his poor cardiac muscle had to swell to almost three times its size to try to keep pumping blood through increasingly occluded blood vessels."

"I see it's also breaking up there," McGowan pointed out, while at the same time chasing a juicy piece of beef back into the center of the plate. "What's that mean when the heart falls apart on you?"

"Well, it could mean a few things, Michael," Gordon answered archly. "It could mean someone with an ice pick performed involuntary closed-chest surgery. But since I was present and didn't observe anything of the kind, we'll rule that out. It could also mean that this formalin substitute the government makes us use doesn't work for beans. And do you know why they made us stop using formalin, incidentally?"

McGowan, having a hefty swig of his bottle of beer, shook his head.

"Because," Gordon raged, "a handful of idiots—and the coroner's trade has no more or no fewer idiots than any other—emulating their great hero, the late Bela Lugosi, decided to make a more potent afternoon cocktail with formalin and some milder form of alcohol. Like that beer you're drinking."

McGowan made a face, but kept drinking. His mouth was hot. The chili was spicy.

"It blew out their livers like snuffing a candle," Gordon related. "So naturally, not wanting to admit that they had done something so stupid, the coroners involved insisted that the formalin had given them cancer. And all the timid little field mice that always come out whenever some-one mentions the deadly 'C' word immediately wrote to their pandering congressmen and the running dogs of Washington made it illegal to protect fragile bodily organs throughout eternity with anything stronger than witch hazel and Dawn dishwashing detergent."

McGowan laughed to see his normally pleasant friend get so worked up. "Cosmo, please. You're starting to sound like Stuart Goodwillie."

"In this day and age any man over thirty-five with a newspaper and three drinks under his belt doesn't have any choice but sound like Stuart Goodwillie!" Gordon roared. He was back to normal in an instant. "How's your drink holding out, by the way? Ready for another beer?"

"Absolutely," McGowan said loudly, finishing the last great gulp from his bottle.

"Are those cold enough for you? We keep them right up against the soles of the customer's feet."

McGowan winced as he always did at the medical examiner's gross jokes. He tolerated them, however, because the lieutenant knew that this was the one place where the usually uptight Dr. Cosmo Gordon could really unwind.

"Okay," McGowan said finally, as they both settled back down. "Now you know how much I hate it when you pull me out of the office to come over here and kill the afternoon eating your gourmet food and drinking your expensive booze, but I assume there is some other reason for this meeting?"

Gordon mastered a gas problem, then nodded his head. "Indeed there is, Michael. I was telling you the reasons why a fixed organ would fall apart in a hospital organ jar. Cooked meat does not hold together as well as raw."

McGowan made a face. "You said something about that before. Just what are you getting at?"

"Look here." Gordon shuffled slightly to one side to give his old friend a look.

McGowan peered uneasily into a small Styrofoam-lined box, saw what lay within, and guessed, "He has a communicator to talk to alien spaceships?"

"That's a pacemaker, Michael," Cosmo said a little testily.

McGowan thumped the top of his fist against his own chest to free a gas bubble, then responded, "Okay,

so he died of a heart attack? Is that what you're saying?"

"No," Gordon responded slowly. "Mannheim Goodwillie died because somehow he took in a large number of microwaves which heated this pacemaker until it
exploded. Look here. This goopy gray substance there
on the side is from the batteries. They also exploded."

"Batteries?" McGowan's eyebrows shot up in surprise. "Is that how these things work? That's pretty
crude technology."

"Not as crude as all that, Michael," Dr. Gordon corrected him. "The batteries are made to last almost two
years without recharging. The recharging process, by
the way, can be done in a cardiologist's office on an
outpatient basis with a large magnetto device that won't
cut or burn the skin in any way."

"Hunh," McGowan commented.

"We're not talking about product failure either here,
Michael," Cosmo continued in a stern, serious voice.
"This was either a tragic accident or . . ."

"Murder!" Jackie said loudly in frustration. "This traffic is absolutely murder! What are you looking at, fella?"
Jackie yelled to the guy in the car next to her. "Just drive
your car."

"Would you calm down already, Maria Andretti?"
Jackie's front-seat passenger complained. "I'm getting
a migraine here listening to you. And it's driving your
dog bonkers too."

"I'm sorry, Millie," Jackie apologized.

Millie Brooks, Jackie's college roommate and her
oldest friend, was the film instructor's best buddy on
the Rodgers faculty.

"And I'm sorry, Jake!" Jackie continued. "It's just that
people are taking the fact that they're on a 'parkway'
too literally. The gas is the one on the right, sir!" Jackie

yelled out her window to the man in front of them.

"Jackie!"

"All right! All right! I won't yell," Jackie promised, crossing her fingers. "Millie, buckle up. Jake, get down off the seat. I am now going to show you just why I bought a Jeep." Jackie pulled off onto the shoulder, then went down the slight incline to a farmer's dirt road paralleling the highway.

"Whoo!" cried Millie delightedly. "Remember when we used to go boy-dodging, driving like this? I wish we had a fifth of Tango Apricot to chug right now."

"It's in the glove compartment," Jackie responded, taking a hand off the wheel for a moment to point. "Jake!"

The big dog stuck his head between the two seats immediately to hear his mistress's communication.

"How you doing, big fella?"

The dog wagged his tail happily. He liked going fast. Jackie did too, the problem was, her long, dark, curly hair was blowing in her eyes.

Millie then yelled in her high, tight voice, "Jackie! I can't find it!"

"It's in there," Jackie yelled back, brushing at her hair again.

"Got it!" Millie then announced, holding up a bottle. "Want to open it with your teeth for old times' sake?"

"That's all right," Jackie said. "Go ahead."

"Okay."

All of a sudden they heard a noise. "Pull over! Pull over!"

Millie sprayed Tango Apricot all over her side of the windshield.

"Great!" Jackie looked into the rearview mirror and saw the familiar gray and orange colors of the strictest highway patrol policemen in the nation. "We're in trouble now."

"Oh, God!" Millie howled. "My dad's gonna kill me."

"Don't get hysterical, Millie," Jackie yelled. "You're thirty-eight years old, remember?"

Millie shook her head. "You don't know my father. He's gotten worse since high school."

Suddenly the loudspeaker voice was heard again. "Speeding, illegal turns at high speeds. Trespassing . . ."

Saying "I know that voice," Jackie jumped out of the car.

Millie and Jake gave each other puzzled looks, then followed her out.

Jackie strode back to the approaching driver of the car behind her.

"And driving under the influence," the voice concluded. "I hope this ticket-writing pen doesn't run out of ink."

Jackie held out her arms. "Ral Perrin! How are you?"

The smiling young teaching assistant embraced her warmly. "Just terrific, thanks to you. I'm settled into my new apartment and you'll be happy to hear I am not contaminating any good neighborhood. I have once again found an apartment on the black side of town."

Jackie shrugged. "According to French scientists, if this greenhouse effect gets any worse, you won't be able to tell us apart."

"Remember I can tan too," Ral pointed out. "If y'all get any darker, we'll just get darker still. Our Miss Brooks! How are you?"

Millie looked blearily at the twenty-seven-year-old cinematographer. "Rascal Ral Perrin. You want to give us all heart attacks?"

"Hey, you weren't doing all that much for the cows' nervous systems, either." Ral waved his arm, indicating a stand of befuddled farm animals a couple of hundred feet away.

"I think those are goats, Ral," Jackie informed him, shading her eyes with her hand.

"Man . . ." the Los Angeleno was impressed. "They're humongous."

"Yeah," Jackie confirmed. "We get 'em pretty big here."

At that, Ral turned to Millie. "You got any of that Tango Apricot left?"

Millie made a face although she knew Ral was probably kidding her. "Ral Perrin. You should be ashamed of yourself, you being a cop and all."

Ral looked puzzled, then glanced back at his car and started laughing. "Oh, no. You thought I was the heat? That's my heap, child. Look at it. Sure, it's an old police car but the words and emblems and stuff are painted over. See? Only cost me a hundred dollars. Runs okay. But the suspension's shot. Just driving the speed limit's like watching a movie in Sensurround."

"But your voice . . ." Millie protested. "We heard . . ."

Ral laughed again. "That came with the tape deck I bought for the car, Ms. Brooks. I goof around with it sometimes just to be funny. Hey, Jackie. What's wrong with your dog?"

Jackie turned with alarm as Jake jumped the farmer's fence and ran toward the bleating farm animals.

"Where's he going, Jackie?!" Millie cried in alarm.

"He's gonna tear their throats out," Ral hazarded. "He's turned wolf."

"No," Jackie replied, realizing what was happening. "Just watch."

As the dark-haired film instructor's fellow educators looked on amazed, her dog of almost two years gathered every one of the goats into a bunch and then got them circling at a smart pace in a tight formation U. S. Grant would have cheered.

They watched for a few moments while Jake led the goats into configurations resembling various algebraic symbols, then all of a sudden he started leading the goats out across the field for a more ambitious stunt.

"What's he doing?" Millie asked.

"Let's find out," Jackie responded, indicating with a jerk of the thumb that they should move to higher ground.

Jackie and Ral helped Millie come up after them as they scrambled up the nearby hill.

"What the heck?" Ral exclaimed when the formation became clear.

Millie was more perplexed than ever. "M?"

"Capital M," Jackie corrected. She didn't know what this meant, but she knew that it was important. "Come, Jake!" she yelled.

The big dog started for them at once.

"Well, this was fun!" Millie announced as she clambered down.

"Just a minute!" Ral said as the two women headed for Jackie's Jeep.

Jackie turned with a questioning look.

Ral gently tugged on Jackie's arm. "I didn't chase you all the way out here just to watch the hick halftime hour."

"So?" Jackie asked.

"I have something for you." Ral walked to his former police car. Jackie followed and the cinematography teaching assistant dug out a black plastic box.

"A videotape?"

"This isn't *Abbott and Costello Go to Mars,* Jackie," Ral said impatiently.

"What is it?"

"The eyewitness!" Ral saw Jackie's puzzled gaze and explained to her, "The dude that checked out. I was taping him, Lady Detective. You're the movie watcher, right? Well, here's your chance to kick back with a bowl of popcorn and figure out who killed Uncle Manny."

CHAPTER 4

For the second time in two days Stuart Goodwillie was holding court in the KJRD radio station's green room.

"I don't understand what we're waiting for," Goodwillie bleated. "Slap this man in irons and set the scaffold builders to work."

Chief Lorne "Hero" Healy, a heavyset, white-haired Irishman with a dark five o'clock shadow and hairy knuckles, tried to calm down the irate millionaire.

"Now, Mr. Goodwillie, I told you when we came down here, we are just going to question Mr. Monahan. We don't plan to perform an arrest."

"Carnero," Goodwillie yelled to his majordomo. "Call David Frost's Production Company. See if they want to do a television show about Palmer's police department called 'Incredible Bunglers!' "

Keith Monahan, who had gotten very little sleep since the whole horror had begun, finally snapped, "Mr. Goodwillie! I am sick and tired of your bullying. I don't know how you got it into your head that this radio station had anything to do with your brother's tragic death, but you're wrong, sir."

Goodwillie's lips curved into a sneer that would have thrilled an Elvis impersonator. "It'll take a better man than you to convince me, Monahan."

"Sir," Monahan pleaded, almost on the verge of a

breakdown. "Would you just try to look at this dispassionately for a moment?"

"Dispassionately—when my brother was murdered, sir?" Goodwillie quivered with sarcastic rage. "My only living relative? How disinterested must I pretend to be? Why don't I have my man there cut off one of your thumbs and see if you can look at the situation with ironic detachment?"

"Now, now," protested the all-but-ignored Healy.

Keith ran his hands angrily down the front of his sweatshirt. "Mr. Goodwillie. The entire radio station— me, most of all—was shocked when your brother keeled over. What possible reason could I or any of my staff have for killing him?"

"Are you telling me," Goodwillie demanded, "that not one of these callus-covered dwarfs that work for you resent the very existence of people far wealthier than they'll ever be?"

Monahan drew himself up and responded, "If there was anyone who felt that way, sir, and felt it strongly enough to actually do murder, the target would have been someone like you."

"My very point!" Goodwillie thundered. "I was too cagey to submit to your torturous grilling, so you smote my poor brother as revenge."

"Sir," Chief Healy couldn't help but interrupt. "You told me not five minutes ago that your brother lived in Florida and that you hadn't seen him face-to-face for over ten years."

"Are you unfamiliar with interstate affection?" Goodwillie growled. "Perhaps you should get an FBI man to explain it to you. Do you have no family feelings at all, man? Were you a foundling raised by apes? Put your hat back on, Healy, your brain cell is freezing."

While Healy was held back from strangling the industrialist by his driver and Felix Cruz, Goodwillie turned his tender attentions back to Monahan.

"We were discussing, sir, the little matter of murder."

"Your brother, Mr. Goodwillie, was ninety-two years old."

"And fit as a Stradivarius fiddle. What's your point, sir?" Goodwillie stamped his feet petulantly. "Have we reached the point where whenever someone figures you've lived long enough he has the right to run microwaves through you like an old piece of Spam?"

"How could we possibly have arranged a heat ray capable of causing your brother's pacemaker to explode?" Monahan demanded.

"Ah, I see you've been briefed."

"Yes, sir," Monahan admitted quickly. "Detective Sergeant Cruz told me the contents of your brother's autopsy. Who told you?"

"I have my man at the medical examiner's office," Goodwillie replied. "I'll leave the solving of the exact details of how you managed to slaughter my poor flesh and blood to Moe, Larry, and Albert Einstein over there. I want nothing more to do with you. My lawyer, however, will soon become your constant nemesis. Nate, tell him."

Dapper Nate Northcote, the tall, dark, mustachioed attorney who handled most of the Goodwillie affairs, withdrew several sheafs of paper. "Keith Monahan, I serve you with these papers to show cause in the civil court as to why you did maliciously and with malice aforethought . . ."

"You're talking too slowly, you idiot." Goodwillie snatched the papers from his lawyer's hand. "Every time you pay a man by the hour—he dawdles." Goodwillie then turned angrily to Monahan and threw the papers in his face. "Read them and weep, Mr. FM. I'll sue you people until this college is a bunch of feed barns."

Monahan turned white-faced with anger. "Mr. Goodwillie. Whatever happened to the presumption of innocence?"

"Whatever happened to an eye for an eye?" Goodwillie

then pointed with his umbrella over Monahan's shoulder and out the window. "Pray tell? What could that gruesome object be?"

Monahan turned and saw the shadow thrown by one of the mighty conning towers. "That's the transmission pole, sir. As you well know."

"You'll notice, gentlemen," Goodwillie raised his voice as he turned to include the three policemen in the discussion, "that the moronic Mr. Monahan didn't say that it was a radio antenna. Oh, no, my friends. Mere radio was too inexpensive for the grandiose Sun King Monahan the Fourteenth here. Tell our Keystone detectives, Mr. Crystal Tubes, what energy form your radio signal takes as it is carried to the next station?"

"Microwaves," Monahan mumbled, suddenly remembering.

Goodwillie brushed his hands together as if ridding himself of dirt. "Slap the shackles on him, gentlemen. If you don't have pressure cuffs big enough, follow me down to my car. I have plenty of sets in the trunk."

Jackie all but held her eyelids open trying to improve her concentration as for the third time she watched the tape Ral had given her. So far she couldn't tell a thing. Especially trying to concentrate while her son drummed on a colander in time to his new Joe Jackson CD.

"Peter!" she yelled finally. Of course there was no response. If the music was being played so raucously that it disturbed, then it was certainly too loud to be heard over.

Jackie got up from the little alcove at the rear of her living room that she euphemistically called her "den," picked up her tea mug, and then made her way to the pulsating Walsh kitchen. Throwing open the door was almost painful.

"Peter!" she yelled.

Peter saw his mother scowl and turned down his boom

box several begrudged notches. "What?"

"Turn that off."

"Oh!" Jackie's red-haired progeny tried to argue, but she was having none of it.

"Off!"

Peter groaned as if someone had stuck a dagger into his entrails and twisted it.

"Just what do you mean," Jackie asked, "playing your box three times louder than we agreed you would *ever* play it in this house? And in the process I see you have beaten my colander completely out of shape."

"What?"

"This," Jackie all but shouted, holding up the dented metal strainer practically to her son's nose. She had found with teenagers that it was easier to get them to take responsibility for themselves if you provided a visual aid.

"You know, Mom," Peter replied, "maybe I'd have turned out better if you didn't yell at me so much."

Knowing all the while that she had no reason to, Jackie felt guilty. "All right. I won't yell. Please don't use kitchen implements as snare drums, Peter. Now if you'll pack up your traveling band equipment I'll start dinner."

"I thought you had your poker game tonight?"

"I do. Your dinner."

"Don't bother," Peter said disgustedly.

"You've got to eat something, Peter, that doesn't come in a little twenty-five-cent bag."

"Leave money," Peter urged. "I'll get a nice nutritious pizza."

"You are having salmon and fruit salad," Jackie said firmly.

"Oh, please . . ." Peter moaned. "If you want to torture me, use a rubber hose."

"That's your dessert." Jackie pushed Peter toward the door. "Now, out!"

"What about child abuse?" he wailed.

"What about parent abuse?" Jackie raged right back. "If I ran this country parents could take their children to court and sue them for cruelty. I'd demand every penny I ever spent on you and ten thousand dollars in damages. You'd be working at Record Shack for the rest of your life to pay me back."

"Yeah, well, I'll let you know when the mental hospital van gets here, Mother."

Jackie turned and started wiping counters. "Honestly," she said to herself. "How do teenage boys who stay in bed all day track in dirt from three or four different places? They must send away for dirt kits from mail-order houses on the back of their comic books."

She had barely gotten dinner started when a loud cracking voice from the living room cried out, "Ma! Can I turn off your tape! So I can watch TV?!"

Jackie opened the swinging kitchen door and looked out to her son, who had dragged down all the pillows from his own bed so in the event he dozed off on the couch he wouldn't feel disoriented.

"You know, sweetheart," Jackie said in a bright cheery voice. "You might find that tape interesting if you sat down to watch it. I've been studying it too. We could discuss it at dinner. It's the actual last moments of a rich industrialist's life."

"Yawn."

So much for making an effort to spend more quality time with your children, Jackie thought to herself. "Okay, just make sure you remember to take my tape out of the TV and put it back in the black plastic tape box."

"*Jawohl, mein Herr!*" Peter yelled.

"Watch that Palmer German-American humor, mister."

As her son goose-stepped around the living room singing "Horst Vessel," Jackie ground her teeth, cursed the

school system for forcing adolescent students to take a
second language, and then went back into the kitchen.

Jackie was still grumbling to herself when she arrived
at her mother's house for their usual Thursday night
meeting of the Ladies Gambling Society.

"Ah, here she is," Frances Costello called out as Jackie
let herself into her mother's old apartment with her key.
"Spawn of my womb, two hours late for her own birth
she was, how can we expect her to be on time for a mere
game of chance?"

"What sort of cutthroat poker are we playing, Mother?" Jackie asked, entering the living room and slinging
her shoulder bag to the couch.

"Spit in the Ocean," Frances responded, riffling the
cards like an expert. "We're dealing the four-card-hold
variation with flushes and straights to be at least six
cards. Should I deal for you? Toss Maggie your wallet.
She'll give you your chips."

Jackie looked at the gathering already surrounding the
table. First there was Maggie Mulcahy, her mother's
oldest friend in the world, a sweet, dark-haired, retired
telephone operator with a great wad of bandages and
cotton affixed to her right ear. Next to her was Frances's
good friend, a pal from her Snake Club, a handsome,
small-boned black woman with a beautiful halo of soft
curly gray hair, Bara Day. Next to Bara was Jackie's
friend Millie, chewing ice cubes to hide her nervousness,
the way she did every poker game, and last, next to
where Jackie would be sitting, was Jean Scott, the canny
white-haired book critic of the Palmer *Chronicle*.

Jackie crossed her arms and fumed, staring directly
into her mother's face.

"Look at me frock, Maggie," Frances instructed. "Do
you see any scorch marks where my daughter is trying
to stare holes in me?"

"Could I have a word with you in the kitchen after

this hand, *Mother!*" Jackie demanded.

"Of course, m'love," Frances called out to her daughter's retreating back. "A mother can never do enough for her only daughter. Don't stand there gaping, Jean Scott, it's unpleasant to those of us who still have all their own teeth. Bara, it's your bet, dear. Live dangerously. We're all old here, what's the point of holding on to it?"

Jackie went into the kitchen that had been her favorite room when she lived in the apartment with her parents so very long ago. She pulled a carafe of white wine out of her mother's closet-sized refrigerator, poured it into a rocks glass, added a slice of lemon and a slice of lime and a tiny splash of Tom Collins from the bar tray, and then rummaged through the finger foods on the kitchen counters still waiting to be brought out.

As Jackie snacked, she could hear all the chatter from the dining-room poker game as clearly as if she were in the same room.

"You didn't make the stuffed bugle crackers, Frances," Millie was saying.

"Get your head out of your soup, Millie, why don't you?" Crabby with her daughter, Frances was taking it out on her guests. "I haven't made those hors d'oeuvres in months. There's a bowl of crackers there next to you big enough to float a battleship. The cans next to 'em are cheese. Spray them any way you like."

"Oh, these are cheese," Millie remarked with some surprise. "I thought they were party favors. You know, the sort of plastic string you squirt on the floor."

"No, it's not," Frances replied testily. "And don't be squirting cheese on the walls or ceiling either. You don't like it, spend eighty-nine cents and bring a bag of corn twists every once in a while, why don't you? Excuse me."

Frances stepped into the kitchen and put her hands together as if delighted. "Jackie, darling. You've done your hair the way I like it—touching up the gray so it doesn't show so badly. Thank you, darling. Who's your hairdresser?"

"Never mind that, Mrs. Attack-First-and-Gain-the-Advantage Frances Cooley Costello."

"Oh, dear!" Frances pressed the back of her wrist to her forehead. "She's mad at her dear mother again. Where's the razor so I can slash me wrists?"

"None of that!" Jackie responded. "How many times . . . ?"

"You know I'm too polite to count, dear . . ."

"*How many times* must I tell you no more than five people at a table for poker?!"

Knowing all this was coming, Frances had her defenses firmly in place. "Open the window there, dear. I beg you. I'll throw myself out and that'll leave you with five."

"Come on, Mother."

"There's no sacrifice," Frances yodeled, "that I wouldn't make for you, my darling!"

Jackie wasn't fooled for a moment. "Mother, I saw you do this play at the Red Barn Community Theater when I was in high school."

"Ah," Frances smiled. "So you do remember every now and then that your mother was an actress? That Lady Dunsany. If you'd written like her, love, you wouldn't have had to go back and teach in the university."

Jackie gave her mother a wry look, knowing full well that Frances could keep changing the subject all evening long. "Thanks, Mom. But I'm one of those female masochists you read about in magazines. Although I could make myself fabulously wealthy with just a snap of my fingers, I insist on living on the edge of poverty while I slog away at a full-time job."

Frances Costello had a ready answer for this one as well. "Marry that policeman fellow, McGilley, or whatever his name is."

"I like Michael, Mother," Jackie replied. "But it's going to be a long time before I think about marrying anyone again. Now, before you start making scurrilous remarks about my complexion . . ."

Frances made her well-I-do-hate-to-tell-you-this-but-since-you-brought-the-subject-up face, but Jackie didn't give her a chance to so much as open her mouth. "Why? Why when we've discussed this so much, did you invite three people when you knew I was bringing Millie?"

"Well, you know, dear"—Frances hung her head miserably—"when you get to be my age, you get so you start to forget things and . . ."

"Don't play Sara Senile with me either!" Jackie snapped.

"Well, now," Frances replied placidly. "I'm glad to see you remember every performance of mine they took you to so clearly. It's a pity I didn't know it at the time when it was my considered impression that you were out front snoring."

"I don't snore, Mother." Jackie drew herself up indignantly. "I have a bit of a sinus problem."

"Ah, yes," Frances snorted. "And Broderick Crawford has a sweet tenor voice, it's just that he's a wee bit hoarse."

Jackie succeeded in controlling her temper, but just barely. "Mother . . . Why is Bara Day here?"

Frances walked over to the champagne punch bowl and poured herself a drink. "Well, dear, you can't blame the poor woman for wanting to be playing a delightful game of pasteboards instead of baby-sitting two huge snakes."

"I know, Mother. But why?"

"Well, it's like this, Jackie." Frances sat down on a stool opposite her daughter. "Poor Maggie has the trouble with her ear. And so she needed someone to drive her here, so . . ."

"Mother," Jackie interrupted. "I can see Maggie not wanting to drive when she had the trouble with her eye, but you can drive perfectly well with one ear . . ."

"Jackie, darling," Frances replied, grabbing her daughter's arm. "It was her good ear. You don't know what it is to go through a life without the reassuring buzz of noise in your ear, to be locked into an endless silent hell . . ."

"Mother." Jackie laughed aloud at her mother's outrageousness. "This is getting to be *Rhino Video Presents the Greatest Hits From the Palmer Abbey Theater.*"

In response, Frances summoned up a little tear.

Jackie sighed. "I'm not going to win this one, am I?"

The tear disappeared at once. "No, dear. Of course not."

"All right then," Jackie surrendered. "We'll make do."

Frances smiled and then asked, "How about a top-off on your beverage, dear? There's still plenty of this delicious whiskey punch."

Jackie watched her mother pour herself a stiff one, then sniffed the air suspiciously. "Mother, don't you think it's time you took out that ham loaf?"

"Oh, so it is," Frances responded, darting a look at the kitchen clock. "Thank you my good, kind, thoughtful daughter."

As her mother worked at the stove, Jackie filled a Fibra-Foam plate with snackables. "Mother! What do you know about Mannheim Goodwillie's murder?"

Frances tugged on her oven mitts. "Just what I read in the papers, dear."

"I'm sure that will be quite enough," Jackie replied, sitting on the stool her mother had vacated. "You read the newspapers more closely than most nonunion proofreaders. Give me the meat."

"Here you are, dear." Frances put a piece of ham loaf on Jackie's plate.

"Yum."

"It does look good, doesn't it?" Frances licked her thumb off, then wiped her hands with a dishcloth. "Now, where shall we start? Well, *The Trib* told us he called himself a chemist, Mannheim Goodwillie did, but in actuality he was a bean counter in charge of a group of talented chemists whose work was patented in his name as part of every employee's contractual agreement."

"I like that one."

Frances gave a glad-to-be-of-service smile and then started folding over pieces of sliced ham roast and skewering them with toothpicks. "The Palmer *Chronicle* chose to speculate on the possibility that Mannheim Goodwillie was the tragic victim of a death ray being secretly tested in the L5 range to prove that the Strategic Defense Initiative was viable."

Jackie shook her head. "The good old *Chronicle*. They shake out their red union suits every morning so they don't get bit by some CIA spider."

Frances continued, "The *Gazette* recalled how Mannheim Goodwillie humiliated Henry Obermaier in the fifties by disclosing that he'd been sent home from the Korean War and discharged as mentally unfit."

"Mannheim Goodwillie is against psychotherapy?" Jackie asked, amazed.

"The Goodwillies," Frances answered as she started to arrange the ham loaves on a serving plate, "were always against anything that kept people from working twelve-hour days. My first beau worked for Falk & Goodwillie when I was still in school. He'd be late for eight o'clock dinner engagements without fail and then fall asleep on my shoulder when we went dancing."

"It's your own fault for leading, Mother," Jackie joked, immediately poising herself to duck in case her mother threw a ham ball at her.

"The *Post-Inquirer*," Frances continued coolly, "disclosed that the break that led to Mannheim Goodwillie's exile in Daytona, Florida, was not voluntary retirement but a tremendous quarrel between the two brothers over a tempestuous city council woman, now the mayor of Pretty Palmer, Jewel Box of Ohio, Jane Bellamy."

"Shudder, gasp."

Frances nodded. "*Cherchez la femme*, says the *Post-Inquirer*, whether there's a woman to be found or no."

"And Joe Caesar's *Real* tabloid?"

Frances nodded grimly. "Palmer's local media lunatic pronounces Mannheim Goodwillie's death to be a hoax. A corpulent body, the late Elvis Presley, Robert Maxwell, or Colonel Sanders perhaps, stolen out of the graveyard, was substituted and now the canny former chemist is holed up in some free banking country like Liechtenstein, cackling to himself about how he duped Uncle Sam's tax bureaucracy out of hundreds of millions."

"They paint a pretty picture," Jackie chuckled.

This casual reaction offended the practical Frances. "Are you daft, child? Colonel Sanders has been dead for fifteen years! How could he possibly still be a corpulent . . . ?"

"I really am kidding, Mother."

"Oh, well," Frances sniffed. "I hope your jokes make you so much money you can afford to live in Castle-Smart-Aleck-in-the-Sky. If you'll rouse yourself and take that tray and that pitcher in I know it'd certainly make the last days of a dying woman a tiny slice better."

The poker game went on uneventfully for more than an hour. Maggie Mulcahy had to sit out every fourth or fifth game due to her pounding, swollen ear. And Jackie had just come back from taking a bathroom break when all of a sudden the bells started clanging.

"Mother! What is it?"

"The warning bell, dear," Frances answered placidly.

Jackie looked around perplexed. "What warning bell? We didn't have warning bells when I lived here."

"Well," Frances shrugged. "There weren't quite so many senior citizens here then either. We made the landlords install the alarm system a few years back so none of us would sleep through a major fire."

"What do we do?" an alarmed Millie asked.

"We call this hand null and void," Frances said decisively. "This way no one will be tempted to peek at the other's cards when we get up from the table. Then we get our jackets and go outside."

"What about Victor?" Jackie asked.

"Victor and *Scalia*," Bara said at once.

"Victor and Scalia, darling," Frances repeated. "Of course Bara brought her Scalia to visit with Victor."

"I can't leave her at home any more than your mother can Victor," Bara pointed out crabbily.

"And they're such a cute couple," Frances simpered.

"Do you think there will ever be a bunch of little snakes?" Millie asked.

"I don't know, dear," Frances replied.

"Maybe we should just get some chairs and sit down and watch them sometime, Francie," Bara suggested.

"It's a thought," Frances agreed.

"The fire, Mother," Jackie reminded Frances impatiently.

"Oh, well." Frances looked a little miffed to be reminded of such an inconsequentiality. "You just go out the door there with me now. We all go to the end of the hall. You take the stairs to the lobby. We're only on the seventh floor here so it's not *so* bad. Maggie's on the eleventh floor where she is. Aren't you, Maggie?"

"Let's go!" Jackie yelled. "Mother, what about the snakes?"

"They'll stay here," Frances replied with a shrug. "Things get a little hot, they won't care. They like it hot."

"Smoky too," Bara Day added.

"Really?" This new fact interested Frances far more than any fire. "I didn't know that."

"Mother! Bara!" Jackie started calling the roll. "Jean! Maggie! Millie! Everybody who doesn't want to be fried to a cinder, follow me."

"She's very bossy," Jean Scott commented to Frances as they scurried out.

"It's my cross to bear," Frances added sadly.

After ninety endless minutes spent nattering, breathing the smoke from Jean Scott's cigarettes (which the elderly book reviewer lit one after another to hide the fact that she was nervous), meeting and being reintroduced to neighbors whose only memory of Jackie was as a pimply-faced, gawky teenager who kept bumping into things (coincidentally, not one of the great times in Jackie's memories), much to Jackie's relief, they arrived back at the apartment door to see two snakes reared up to a full seven feet and staring down at them as if they were giant dragons guarding the desert wizard's pavilion.

"Isn't that cute?" Frances said. "Our babies missed their mommies."

"What the heck are you talking about, you old coot?" yelled Bara. "They've got something trapped."

Sure enough, as the women crowded into the room they found a mutt, part Doberman, part Dalmatian, a dog that could attack or retreat fast, cowering in the corner.

"How did he get in here?" Millie asked.

"I left the door open," Frances responded. "I'd rather not have the firemen breaking down my door if I can help it."

"You know, I'll bet whoever it is counted on that," Jackie said.

"What are you talking about?" asked the already-nervous Jean Scott as she agitatedly took her package of cigarettes out of her bag.

"I know what he's here for," Jackie exclaimed. She then walked to her bag and fished out the videotape box. Jackie held it over, brought it closer, and the burglar dog nervously tried to clasp it in his teeth.

"Someone trained a dog to come in here and steal your videotape?" Maggie asked, amazed.

Jackie nodded and said, "I've got a feeling this is just the beginning."

CHAPTER 5

While Ivor Quest—the distinguished motion picture director turned chairman of the Communications department—paced back and forth, his faculty sat respectfully in their chairs at the oblong meeting table that had been snapped up when the Palmer Regular Steel Company went out of business.

"Friends," Quest began, forcing his tanned, face-lifted features into a wide, disarming smile. "This department has had its share of tragedies. One murder victim. Two murderers. And one of you has been menaced . . . What—how many times has it been, Jackie?"

"Four as of last night," the tired film instructor replied.

"There we are," Quest nodded. "Most of us here have been a suspect in one murder or another. Is there anyone here who hasn't been a suspect?"

Fred Jackson's hand went up at once.

"Yes, well, of course, Fred. The only shooting he does is with his camera, right?"

Fred Jackson, the bon vivant cinematography instructor, and also the co-deputy department chairman, who had gladly taken the Ed McMahon role to Ivor Quest's Johnny Carson, roared with laughter.

The laugh, however cheaply won, pleased Quest. He continued, "Now we have another crisis. Keith Monahan, our Radio Arts instructor, is in jail. For a murder he didn't commit, we'd all like to think, right?"

There was a smattering of applause.

"Jackie Walsh has proposed," Quest continued, shooting his silk cuffs, "and I agree, that we all come out strongly for Keith. Many a murderer has gone free in this part of the country because he was popular in his community. We should consider that. And of course, if our Mr. Monahan actually didn't do it, then the poor man really should be freed."

There was another round of applause, stronger than the last but far from enthusiastic.

Quest sighed, thinking as he did at least once a day that it was a shame to be a genius unappreciated in his own time. "Yelena, you've put some thought and effort into organizing this impromptu benefit for Keith Monahan. Why don't you tell us exactly what is happening so far?"

Yelena Gruber, the temperamental Hungarian acting instructress, stood creakily. She then looked fondly at the department chairman, who was a veritable god to her. When the awkward silence became unbearable, she started ticking things off on her fingers. "Some magicians we've got. Ronald Dunn, the actor who Jackie was good enough to contact, will come. I will do a little bit of *Sorry Wrong Number*."

"Oh, really?" Ivor Quest exclaimed. "How wonderful. That's one of my favorites."

Yelena nearly passed out with happiness at her lucky choice. To think, she had been thinking of doing *The Monkey's Paw*. "Jackie and Celestine Barger," she continued happily, "have written a piece that will be performed by Jackie's mother, Frances Costello, and her dog Jake."

"Wonderful, wonderful," Ivor Quest beamed. "And I have just gotten word from my capable secretary that one of the students, Lyn Fevre, will tap dance for us."

"Tap dance?!" Fred Jackson exclaimed loudly. "This is radio! Who's going to know if she's really dancing or if the engineer is just tapping his watch with a pencil?"

Quest turned to his semisidekick, a little more impatiently than usual. "Well, Fred, when one sees a modern movie that takes place in the forties, how does one know that the director didn't just unearth some forgotten film from that period? When you're watching a murderer on the stage, how do you know that he is an actor and not some actual murderer? We must follow the dictates of common sense. Performance art requires an initial leap of faith."

"Besides," Mark Freeman, the roly-poly animation instructor, chimed in, "Fred Astaire used to dance on his radio show every week. Nobody ever accused him of faking."

"Uncle! Uncle!" Fred cried, holding up his hands. "Remind me to never again venture an opinion on any subject other than my own."

"Very well," Quest smiled. "We intend to hold you to that, Fred. So! There's our entertainment package. The Music department has volunteered both performers and tapes. Fred and myself will grant interviews on our glorious careers." Quest paused for the now-anticipated tepid applause, then resumed, "David Surtees and Mark Freeman will lend a hand on the technical end, and Marcus Baghorn, currently in Niagara Falls with his lovely bride, the former Amy Pummer, will fax us publicity material to distribute, when, of course, he's up to it. Are there any questions?"

Suki Tonawanda, Jackie's former TA, now elevated to full instructor status, held up her hand. "Excuse me, Mr. Quest . . ."

"Ivor, please," the charming ex-film director insisted. "Whenever I hear 'Mr. Quest' I always fear I'm about to be served with a subpoena."

"Ivor . . ." Suki started again. "What about the classes? The students?"

The motion picture great made a face. "Yes. To be sure our little wards must continue to have their heads filled with stuff and nonsense. We'll cover our own classes as much as we can, and cover for each other in our own homey Rodgers style."

"In other words," Fred Jackson boomed, "we let the TAs handle things."

"Right you are, Fred. As always," Ivor responded, effortlessly lifting his voice loud enough to drown out even the barrel-chested cinematographer. "Well, we have our missions, then. Let us get cracking. Class dismissed."

As Jackie started for the door, the chairman stopped her. "Miss Walsh?"

"Yes, sir?"

Quest moved quickly to her side. "Would you walk with me a moment?"

Jackie nodded and as her fellow faculty fell wolf-like upon the strudel Yelena Gruber had brought from Klingelhoffer's Kakes, a local bakery, the two strolled to Jackie's new office.

"Miss Walsh . . ." Quest began.

"Yes, Ivor?" They walked to the wide twisting staircase donated from a soon-to-go-bankrupt Hollywood studio, and started slowly up.

"Tell me. Do you intend to take your usual active role in solving this case?"

Jackie, not knowing quite how to answer, replied simply, "I don't know."

"I wish you would get involved, you know." Quest slowed as they got to the top, forcing Jackie to look back at him.

"Really? Why?"

Quest smiled, then put his hand on his sternum as if to say he was out of breath. Jackie nodded and she brushed her identification badge against the electric eye opening the door to her office. Quest immediately sank

into her blue director's-style visitor's chair and sighed
with relief.

Jackie switched on her desk light, briefly checked
her computer screen to confirm that there weren't any
messages, then sat on her own white vinyl editing stool
with its flexible back that gave Jackie support no matter
how she contorted herself in her seat. "You're getting out
of shape, Ivor," she joshed.

"Nonsense," the dazzling septuagenarian smiled back
at her. "I was never in shape. What do we brilliant
people care for muscle tone?" He then tapped the arms
of his chair. "This is very comfortable, by the way.
Oddly enough, you know, it's the first time I've ever
sat in one."

"Really?" Jackie was amazed. "Are you kidding me?"

"No, no," the elderly director assured her. "For my
pictures, you know, I sat on the crane, mostly. Or paced
round waiting for the assistants to flog the extras into
place. When I first started out I requested wooden
campaign chairs. It's what I'd seen Livingstone and
Hitchcock use in England when I was their assistant
and I thought they were de rigueur."

"Well," Jackie smiled. "It's always here when you
want to come visit."

"How nice. Thank you." Quest smiled again, giving
Jackie the unmistakable impression that the chances that
he would be a frequent visitor to her small office were
almost too negligible to measure. "I know you're busy,
Jackie. So I'll come right to the point. Thanks in large
part to your commendable efforts, Stuart Goodwillie and
his brother were persuaded to loosen their purse strings
and once again contribute to the university. It was an
unexpected blessing. After the tainted water episode I
thought we'd lost him forever but you . . ."

"Blackmailed him into financing the new Radio Arts
Building," Jackie filled in.

Quest smiled. "There is undoubtedly a more elegant

way of putting it, but since the words were yours, I won't quibble with them. The problem, baldly put, Jackie, is this: although the building proper is complete, there are the inevitable bits and dabs that still need doing. Some of the contractors have not yet submitted their bills. Some have only been paid in part. The amount of money still outstanding, which the Goodwillies are still morally bound to pay, is not small. If Stuart Goodwillie refuses to settle whatever debts still remain, the creditors will, it goes without saying, come after us."

"Uh-oh," Jackie responded.

"To be sure," Quest agreed, now becoming quite serious. "I'm sure in time the questions would be settled in some tedious legal forum and that things would eventually resolve themselves. However, it would cast a great gray pall on the excitement attendant in showcasing our new building. It would mean mixed or bad publicity in the local newspaper and television networks, and whatever hope we had of using this new addition to attract a flood of new tuition-bearing students would be quite firmly quashed."

"I understand."

"Yes." Quest nodded, then loosened his ascot slightly, so he could rub the back of his neck. "I considered bringing up the matter at our faculty meeting, but with poor Keith Monahan in the local jail, this is really not the time for it and frankly none of the others can do all that much to help. Only you."

"Me?" Jackie was taken aback. When she had poked her nose into the death of the former Communications department chairman, Philip Barger, she had never anticipated that this would eventually lead to such steady work. "I'd sure love to help, Ivor, but just because I've had some luck helping the police solve murders doesn't mean I'll have any luck this time. I mean, this time I wasn't even there."

"Well," Quest responded, more than a little bit impatient by this time, "you weren't exactly 'Janey on the Spot' all the other times, either, Ms. Walsh. No one says that you have to physically stumble over the carrion before you're able to show any interest. What I need you to do . . ."

"Yes, Chairman Quest," Jackie replied humbly.

Her tone succeeded in lightening the older director's mood. "You must forgive me, Jackie. I'm acting as if I'm directing *War and Peace* again and ordering Napoleon around."

"That's all right, Ivor," Jackie smiled. She really did like her chairman and knew that there must be times when the Hollywood legend wondered if he'd done the right thing to pass up a graceful retirement to come all the way out here and chair a controversial Communications department. "What would you like me to do?"

"Politic a bit, Jackie," Quest responded. "I humbly request on behalf of rugged old Rodgers U. that you talk to former President Obermaier; the medical examiner, Dr. Gordon; Her Honor, Mayor Bellamy; the pearl of the Palmer press, Ms. Jacobs; and the questionably sane Mrs. Blue . . ."

Jackie smothered a smile. She knew that for the professionally charming Chairman Quest to be openly critical of anyone, Alice Blue must have been making Quest's life a living hell.

"Question them," Quest instructed, "as you think appropriate, about what they saw and what they may know about the killing of Mannheim Goodwillie. At the same time, feel them out. See what they feel toward the university. Animosity? Hostility? Do they hold us responsible or can we go to them if Mr. Goodwillie refuses to meet his obligations . . . ?"

"If he welches," Jackie clarified.

Quest favored her with a bemused smile. "Such a lovely word, yes. And so appropriate. If he 'welches,' Miss Walsh, will we have a sympathetic mayor and press

to take our case to or will our former president and some
lunatic band sympathetic to a two-time murderess kick in
our ribs as we lay helpless on the ground?"

"You have a way with a phrase yourself," Jackie
responded.

"I've always stolen from the best writers of my day,"
Quest smiled. "Will you help us?"

Jackie's response was paired with a smile that matched
exactly the smile on the poster of Mae West that decorated the film instructor's one unobstructed wall. "Of
course."

The fabulous Bellamy mansion was located in the
fashionable South Side District of Palmer. From the
outside, the house looked perfectly normal. Like the
Amityville house, for instance. Jackie saw a sign on
the ornate front door that said, "Come On In."

The dark-haired instructor grasped the door knocker
that looked, strangely enough, like a brass pig's foot, and
tapped it a couple of times just to make sure. Receiving
no response, Jackie proceeded inside.

The interior of the Bellamy house was all polished
floors, gleaming silver, and heavy cedar furniture. It
reminded Jackie a little of the German girls' school in
Maedchen im Uniform. Jackie followed the regimentally
arranged orange and black party favors down the hall.
Mayor Jane Bellamy had told Jackie that it was her
daughter Maureen's birthday.

As Jackie walked down the corridor that apparently
led to a parlor of some sort, she noticed the pictures
on the wall. First up were pictures of Jane as she was
when singing in the local opera. Next came pictures
of the young Jane with her handsome young doctor
husband, Dick. As Jackie proceeded down the corridor the pictures changed to depict a later time in their
lives, when the proud mother and father had first a
little girl and then a little baby boy. From there the

pictures recounted the children's lives, climaxing with high school graduation pictures. Then there came a small set of pictures of the two Bellamys alone. First there was Dick Bellamy, still looking boyish, now a surgeon and hospital administrator at the Marx-Wheeler Hospital. Then came photos of Jane Bellamy as Jackie first knew her, as an austere, frighteningly intelligent university professor at Rodgers, teaching City Planning at the Business school. Last, just before she arrived where she wanted to go, Jackie saw pictures of the Bellamy inaugural featuring the second set of children that the Bellamys had acquired, their adopted children, Maureen and Kevin.

Jackie reached the open parlor door and slowly walked inside. So conditioned was she to seeing Jane Bellamy in one exquisitely tailored European suit after another that when the mayor turned to her, dressed in a clown suit, Jackie almost screamed.

"Jacqueline," gushed the clown. "Welcome to our beautiful home."

When Jane Bellamy brought up her hand from where it had been hidden behind her back, Jackie sighed with relief to see that it did not contain an ax. "Thank you," Jackie replied, shaking Jane's hand, "for having me, Your Honor."

"Please," the mayor protested insincerely, "Jane is fine. This mayoral courtesy, much as I enjoy it, I never allow to flourish over that doorsill. I am and always will be," Mayor Bellamy gushed, "*Jane* to my friends."

Jackie nodded noncommittally.

The mayor then raised her voice to a pitch that could crack ice. "It's my Maureen's birthday party!" She then swung her white-gloved hands toward a beautifully dressed little Dresden doll of a person. "Maureen, say hello to Miss Walsh, dear."

"Hello," Maureen responded quickly.

Jane stood over her adopted daughter, her painted harlequin features contorted into a smiling grimace. "My little Maureen is not squirming around and mussing up her new party dress, is she?"

"No, Mommy dearest," Maureen replied with a sweet little smiling grimace of her own.

Jackie could see from the combed velour cushions next to her little makeup-covered legs and the brushed satin rug beneath her tight, black-polished, little shoes that Maureen had not moved for some time. She wondered if the little girl was in pain.

"Let's go into my office, shall we? We won't be disturbed in there." Jackie flinched again as Jane turned her eerie grease-painted countenance toward her. Somehow the mayor's eyes, surrounded by sharp red triangles, unsettled Jackie.

"Fine!" she blurted out.

"She's such a good girl," Jane smiled down at her daughter again. "We're going to have a photographer from City Hall here shortly. My little Maureen photographs so divinely and of course we have a complete photographic record."

Jackie shuddered again, noticing that the mayor's lipstick, under her clown white makeup, was brilliant and bloodred. "You're having the City Hall photographers shoot a child's birthday party?"

"You don't approve?" Jane replied lightly. "Is this where all corruption starts? When you have photographs taken of a personally significant event?"

It's just, Jackie thought to herself, *that we already have enough photographs of clowns in City Hall*—but she said, "It's so unusual."

"I thrive on the unusual," Jane announced. Then, giving one of her daughter's braids a not unpainful tug by way of saying good-bye, the mayor led Jackie through the bookshelves into another smaller room.

The door creaked open and as soon as Jackie could get inside, it mysteriously slammed shut. Jane walked to her desk, kicked off her oversize shoes, and took off her bright red fright wig (revealing thin orange-dyed hair clipped painfully close to the skull). "Sit down!" she said gaily.

Jackie flung herself into a guest chair.

The mayor sat as if settling on an egg, then gave Jackie a kind of dazzling smile. "Children are such a challenge, don't you think? Maureen and little Kevin, who you haven't met yet"—Jane's hand alit on a large framed desk picture of little Kevin, who was perfectly posed—"are adopted. With our children off in prep school, we missed the marching of little feet and so we plucked these poor children out of their unhappy home and brought them here to our comfortable one." Jane finished with a smile that gave Jackie gooseflesh.

"But you didn't come here to discuss the Family Services Office with me," Mayor Bellamy pointed out. "What can I do for you, Jackie?"

Still a little nonplussed, Jackie choked out, "Just a few questions about yesterday afternoon."

"Of course."

A faint knock on the wooden door behind her caused Jackie to jump in her chair.

Jane looked up slightly. "What is it, Heinz?"

Jackie turned to see the Bellamy butler, a smirking midget, holding a business card. "The photographers have arrived, madam."

"Prepare the child," Jane instructed. After the butler had departed, the mayor turned back to her guest. "Which reminds me. How is your child?" The mayor consulted an index card. "Peter? Age twelve?"

"He's not quite twelve yet," Jackie smiled.

"No?" Unpleasantly surprised, Jane at once corrected the card in fierce purple ink. "His hobbies are 'hockey, Nintendo, and playing Frisbee with Jake,' aren't they?"

Jackie nodded.

The mayor put away her card.

"You certainly have a lovely home . . ." Jackie started.

Jane nodded curtly. "It would be sheer colossal impertinence if I thought I could run a city when I couldn't even run my own house."

Jackie nodded, seeing her point, but not wanting to give the mayor an opening. If there was one area that Jackie did not want to compete with Jane Bellamy in, it was running the well-ordered home.

"How is Dr. Bellamy?" Jackie asked, somewhat stalling for time, but also wanting to hear the mayor answer routine questions, so she could judge later if changes came into Jane's voice.

"Dick Bellamy continues to be the most handsome, most capable, most brilliant plastic surgeon and hospital administrator in Palmer history. But of course I'm prejudiced. Have you ever been to Marx-Wheeler Hospital? Is there a more perfect medical center anywhere?"

Jackie shook her head.

"Of course not. I could never tolerate an imperfect husband. How is . . . ?" Again Jane Bellamy consulted an index card. "Michael McGowan, a handsome, dark-haired lieutenant in the Homicide Bureau of the Palmer police department?"

"He seems to be well," Jackie replied, forcing another smile.

"Police lieutenant. Homicide. Yes. Now, I see." The mayor snapped her card back into its folder. "You are wondering if I had anything to do with the murder of Mannheim Goodwillie. How serious a suspect am I?"

"Well . . ."

"Don't pull your punches. I can take it." Jane Bellamy, in fact, looked like she could take anything, chew it up and spit it back in the face of the person who had dished it out to her.

"Actually, Jane," Jackie waffled, "at this point the police just want to know who saw what and try to figure out what happened."

"Well, I can tell you right away what I saw and"—Jane leaned forward conspiratorially—"this may surprise you, Jackie."

The dark-haired instructor leaned forward expectantly.

This was the mayor's cue to lean back abruptly in her own chair. "Nothing! I saw nothing! Do you know why?"

Jackie shook her head.

Jane reached into a leather case and pulled out a pair of gold-rimmed reading glasses. "I was wearing these! Magnifiers for small print. I wanted to review my speaking material which I had written on several tiny cards. When I wear these, I can't see three feet beyond my face. You have excellent vision, I'm sure. Do you want to see for yourself?"

Jackie shook her head at the proffered spectacles. She believed the mayor. "Did you by any chance hear anything?"

"What was that?" Jane asked pleasantly. "I didn't hear the last thing you said, darling. I'm a little hard of hearing."

As if to prove the last statement, Heinz the butler opened the door and said in a loud voice, "Sorry to interrupt, Madame, but the photographer said to tell you that he is having trouble with your daughter."

Jackie watched Jane's long fingers arch and her nails dig into the arms of the chair like talons. "Oh, he is, is he?" The mayor's nostrils flared and when she could speak again, Jane's voice was tight with anger. "Tell the man I will put an end to that."

The mayor then rose ominously from her chair. "Jackie, dear!" Jane gave her guest a sidelong look. "Duty calls. We are through here, aren't we?"

"Well . . ."

"Sorry I couldn't be more help," Jane lied. "If that darling policeman friend of yours wants to talk with me further, tell him he can always find me during work hours at City Hall. He should call ahead, of course, so my attorney can sit in. Such a bother murder investigations are, don't you think? But of course you're a veteran of these things and I'm just a blushing amateur." Then, with a wide smile, Jane Bellamy stalked from her room.

Jackie started to collect her things when she saw Heinz standing at the door waiting for her. "Yes?"

"I will see you out."

"Oh, that's all right. I can find my way."

Heinz smiled icily. "The madam insists I see every guest out personally."

Jackie took a last look around and shivered. It was then that she recognized that the room she was in had once been a conservatory. All of the paraphernalia had been removed, however, and now there was nothing living in the room whatsoever.

CHAPTER 6

Jackie's next destination was a familiar stopping place. The Blue home, not surprisingly a small colonial home with blue trim, was the scene of much activity these days. Alice, whose son Bobby played on the hockey team with Peter, had gotten involved with the Committee to Free Merida Green and the crusade now took up most of her waking hours.

Passing under a sign that said "Free Merida Now" Jackie made her way down the long sidewalk that led to the Blue backyard. The front entrance was blocked by plastic-covered pallets of boxed appliances that Ford Blue sold at his hardware store.

When Jackie arrived in the backyard, she found herself in the middle of a Folding-the-Mailers Party. Jackie noted a hibachi laden with potatoes, walnut burgers, and tofu franks for the vegetarian barbecue, as a dedicated group of women folded flyers using the edges of heavy bricks.

"Jackie!" Nora yelled. Nora Santucci was the hockey coach's wife and a friend of civil liberties. Thanks to Nora, every hockey player's jersey during last year's disastrous 3–49 year schedule sported memorial Sacco and Vanzetti patches.

"Hello, Nora," Jackie smiled. "Hello, everybody."

The other jolly workers, ready to follow Nora's lead and be nice to Jackie, quickly shifted gears when their leader emerged from her house with a big tray with sponges, bowls of water, and a hundred fifty dollars' worth of stamps donated by a local baker who feared losing the committee members' business to a super-market.

"Jackie Walsh. What are *you* doing here?" Alice asked frostily.

"Oh, just stopped by for a chat," Jackie replied cheeri-ly. "So, how have you been?"

"The Committee to Free Merida Green has done very well," Alice coolly responded. "No thanks to you. We have"—Alice put down the tray in front of a young, unmarried bank clerk pathetically eager to be of service, and then lit up a long, tapered cigarette—"aligned our-selves with the Organization to Take Cigarette Machines out of Pizza Parlors on a quid pro quo basis."

"No cigarettes in exchange for free murderers?" Jackie questioned, unable to help herself.

"That's just what I mean!" Alice set upon Jackie, putting her tense, hate-filled face so close that the dark-haired instructor had to withdraw to avoid getting ciga-rette ashes on her chin. "You're just not a serious per-son."

"What I've come to talk to you about," Jackie replied calmly, "is serious. Mannheim Goodwillie was mur-dered, Alice."

Alice remained predictably dry-eyed. "I can hardly wait to see you try to pin this one on Merida. But, of course, you and your kind have given her a perfect alibi."

Jackie set her own jaw and continued as if Alice hadn't spoken. "Now I can understand that you might not want to talk to me, but you will have to talk to someone. You might find it easier just to chat with me for a few moments than go through the ordeal of a police interrogation. I had to go down to the police precinct and be questioned in one of those little rooms and it's no fun, believe me."

"Let me get this straight," Alice snapped. "You think I should talk to you, because I'm more likely to get a fair deal from you than any police officer? Gee, I don't know, girls. What do you think? Maybe I should ask Merida about that one, hunh?"

Alice's coworkers, who had been clearly signaled that it was safe to laugh, did so.

"What's your point, Alice?" Jackie asked.

"No, no. Nothing, Jackie dear," Alice responded. "It's just that the last time Merida stopped by for a little chat with you she ended up serving life imprisonment."

"All right"—Jackie held up her hand—"that's enough."

"What's the matter?" Alice mocked, her hands on her hips. "Am I making you feel guilty or something?"

"No, Alice," Jackie replied levelly. "I really can't say that I feel guilty. Especially since the woman tried to kill me."

"I don't remember any trials for attempted murder here in Palmer, Jackie," Merida responded archly. "Are you quite sure you haven't been drinking some tainted water?"

Inexplicably, citizens of Palmer were now buying at their local hardware stores five-gallon drums of tainted water salvaged from various city water tanks. Sold for several dollars under such names as Classic Palmer H_2O, the water was snapped up as soon as they could put it out by teenagers convinced the water would get them "high," cooks who claimed cakes just didn't rise as well with the new water, and environmentalists such as Alice Blue, who believed that artificial purifiers weren't safe and that the original anything was better.

"Alice," Jackie responded, "Merida killed two people. She sneaked into my house with a gun."

"Which!" Alice yelled confidently, "she had on her person because she feared for her life. After all, hadn't the previous chairman of her department been brutally murdered?"

"By her!" Jackie practically screamed. "By *her*!"

"So they'd like you to believe!" Alice thundered. "Remember when that chemist testified that prussic acid put in a bottle of hazelnut liquor would turn the drink bright green?"

"Maybe Philip Barger thought he was drinking creme de menthe," Jackie answered.

"There are plenty of other suspects," Alice continued, as if Jackie hadn't spoken. "What about that burglar that menaced your house?"

"The police decided . . ." Jackie abruptly decided she wouldn't play anymore. "Alice, I think what you are doing is at best pointless. Merida Green has been convicted for two murders . . ."

"One murder!" Alice interjected. It was true. The district attorney had never brought anyone to trial for the killing of Danielle Sherman.

"You are not only trying to free someone who doesn't deserve to be freed," Jackie continued. "You're trying to set loose someone who may be very dangerous to all of you and to others."

Alice sniffed loudly at this very real possibility. "Had you bothered to read our literature or check with the Rice Hill authorities, Jackie, my love, you would have found out that Merida Green has been a model prisoner since her very first day in the penitentiary."

"Yes," Jackie responded. "It proves what criminologists keep saying—murderers usually leave each other alone and wait until they can get their hands on someone more helpless."

Alice had run out of words. She held up a pointing finger. "Please go."

Jackie looked around her at the unsympathetic faces and left.

● ● ●

That evening, after a lovely arroz con pollo dinner cooked by Nancy Gordon, Jackie, Jake, and Cosmo Gordon walked through the quiet streets of his suburban development.

"Try not to let it get you down, Jackie," Cosmo urged her.

Jake stopped to give Gordon and Jackie a questioning look. The big dog felt protective about his mistress and did not like to see her unhappy.

"I'm not wildly discouraged," Jackie responded. "I went to see Jane Bellamy and Alice Blue first because I had the feeling they would be the most difficult interviews, but I really don't think I came away with anything."

"You came away with a lot, Jackie," Cosmo corrected her.

"Such as?"

While his mistress and the medical examiner talked, Jake inspected one of the wooden pillars holding up a bus shelter.

"Obviously both women knew something they aren't telling," Cosmo replied.

"Why do you say that?" Jackie asked.

The medical examiner, cleaning his nails with a small blade from his pocketknife as they walked, responded, "Well, for one thing I was sitting five feet from Jane Bellamy. She didn't have those glasses on the entire time, and when she did, Jane kept looking over the tops to see what else was going on. I've known her slightly for almost fifteen years. Her husband's an old friend. Jane has her peculiarities, there's no doubt about that. But she doesn't miss much of what's going on around her. If she does have vision or hearing problems, of which by the way I've heard nothing about before today, Jane more than makes up for it with her network of spies. There are hundreds of people at the university, in city government, in the Palmer business community that Jane has had in one of her business classes or has helped in some way. She keeps in touch with almost every one of them, and they tell her quite a lot. You can be sure of that."

"So why do you think she lied to me?" Jackie asked.

Cosmo shrugged. "Maybe she really didn't see anything. Chances are she wanted to hear from you what the police know and don't know."

A little tired of standing on one spot for so long, Jackie urged Jake on, although the big dog was clearly not finished with his investigations.

"What's the matter?" Cosmo asked, a little irritated about the distraction.

Jackie tugged a little harder on Jake's collar. "He's gotten fascinated by something on this post here."

"It's like a paperback book to him," Cosmo commented.

"All right, all right," Jackie urged the dog. "That's enough for one night. You're going to get nose strain."

As Jake allowed his mistress to slowly drag him away from the site of his investigations, Cosmo commented, "You know, I wonder if he smells Matt?"

Jackie was thrown momentarily. "I beg your pardon?"

"Matt Dugan. His former owner . . ." Cosmo explained.

"Yes?"

Cosmo gestured with his knife blade. "That was the bus stop I walked him to the last time he came out here."

Cosmo was quiet for a moment. Jackie took his arm and they resumed walking.

"When are you going to stop blaming yourself for his death, Cosmo?"

"Oh, probably in twenty years or so. And if you listen to that wife of mine, she'll tell you that the way I treat this old body, it's not likely to last me through the winter."

"Now, now."

"Jackie . . ." Cosmo stopped and she looked up into his face. "There's not a day that goes by that I don't think of Matt."

Jackie nodded.

"So how are things going with you and Michael?"

"*Comme ci comme ça*," Jackie replied quietly.

Cosmo gave Jackie a troubled look. "What's the matter? He too tied up with his work again to spend any time with you?"

"No, actually it's me this time. I'm . . . not sure what I want right now, Cosmo."

The gray-haired medical examiner nodded his head. "Relationships are difficult. Especially when other people are involved. Nancy and I have been having our problems lately."

"Oh, no," Jackie exclaimed. "You two can't divorce. You're the model couple."

"Well, don't put that on us," Cosmo said quickly. "And we're not talking about getting lawyers or dueling pistols yet. It's just that, frankly, Jackie, and this is to go no further, I'm thinking of getting out."

"Quitting the medical examiner's office, you mean?" Jackie asked.

Cosmo nodded. "I've lost the fire in my belly, Jackie. Maybe it will return someday. I don't know. I'd love to just leave Palmer for a while. Sell the house. With Kathy-Elaine gone we don't need all the clutter. I'd like nothing better than to go back to Saskatchewan. Work out of one of the hospitals again. Maybe open a lab or do some consulting work. I think we have enough put aside that I won't have to work so hard. Palmer is changing, Jackie. It's becoming more of a metropolis. That's probably a good thing for a town. But it's not a good thing for a medical examiner. I've seen all the ravages of this violent age that I want to see."

Jackie nodded. "What does Nancy say?"

Cosmo sighed. "She's dead set against a move right now. Loves the town. Loves our life. Hates the idea of starting over and being a frontier doctor's wife in a land where there's snow on the ground six months a year."

"Isn't there a compromise the two of you can make?" Jackie asked.

"We're thinking of a trial separation," Cosmo confessed. "I'll go up for a while. Take an apartment. Scout out the prospects and see if it's really what I want to do. If it is, then I come back and collect Nancy and she tries it for a while. If she can stand it, then we sell the house and start over. If not, then . . ."

Jackie nodded.

"Well, how did we get into that?" Cosmo asked. "Back to the affair at hand." He stepped up the pace and Jake had to hurry to keep up with them. "We were talking about Jane Bellamy."

"You were thinking that she may have seen something," Jackie prompted.

Cosmo nodded briefly. "Whether or not she actually glimpsed something happening at the radio station, Mayor Bellamy knows where the Goodwillie bodies are buried."

"You think so?"

"I'm quite sure of it, Jackie," Cosmo averred vigorously. "She and her investigators have been sniffing around for ages. As you undoubtedly realize, Stuart Goodwillie's promise at the docks to invest his millions in Palmer social programs hasn't resulted in anything more concrete than a few coupon books donated to the senior citizen homes good for a free bottle of Goodwillie Good Water if you buy two at the regular price."

Jackie had heard something to this effect. She was amazed, as usual, that the city had let a felon go free on some vague promise to do better, then, as usual, done nothing to follow up and see that what had been promised was actually carried out.

"Then you think it's possible," Jackie asked, "that it happened the way Stuart Goodwillie said, that someone tried to kill him but accidentally killed Mannheim instead?"

"Anything's possible," Cosmo replied. They turned up the block where Gordon lived. "You coming back in for a cup of coffee? Maybe Nancy has some homemade gingerbread cookies around."

"No." Jackie lightly tapped her hands to her hips. "I'm off the homemade cookies for a while. Besides, I should go home. Peter's there alone. Just one more thing."

"Yes, dear?" Cosmo asked as he bent down to give Jake a good-bye pat.

"What was it I said that made you think Alice Blue was holding back? I mean, she was holding back everything really and didn't want to talk to me at all—but what did you get from that that I'm missing?"

"I'm betting," Cosmo replied, straightening up again, "that if anyone saw anything at all in the studio that day it was Ms. Blue. She arrived late, after everyone else was seated. Whoever operated whatever device that shot microwaves into poor Mannheim Goodwillie's chest must have done it from somewhere behind us, shooting over our heads. We guests were in the so-called bullpen facing the desk set. Keith Monahan and Mannheim Goodwillie were facing each other and since the young lad with the camera—"

"Ral Perrin."

Cosmo nodded. "—had set up quartz lights pointing at them, it was unlikely they could see much of what was happening out in the audience. I have no idea what Alice Blue may or may not have seen, but it strikes me that it would be in her best interests to come forward with any information she might have."

"Why?"

"Well, it proves that murderers are running around Palmer besides her friend Ms. Green for one thing. Plus, it takes the heat off of Ms. Blue herself. As long as she is a suspect in a killing she is personally limited in her effectiveness as an advocate for another murderess. Finally, if Ms. Blue can pull off the sort of coup that you've managed several times now, to lead the police to the murderer, she can generate all sorts of favorable publicity for herself and her cause."

"I guess that's true," Jackie said slowly.

"Of course it is!" Gordon said vehemently. "You don't realize because you've gone out of your way to avoid it, but there's all sorts of ways you could exploit your discoveries. In the situation you and Alice Blue are in now, the person that solves the crime will win the gratitude of the police department, the mayor's office, the university and the radio station, the press, and the medical examiner. That would be an awful lot of weight to throw behind some favorite cause."

"I'm beginning to see your point," Jackie remarked, opening the side door to her Jeep so Jake could jump in. "What if she does know something? Will she sit on it for a while?"

"Perhaps," Cosmo ruminated. "Or maybe she just won't tell you."

"Because I ratted on her pal Merida, you mean?"

"No," the medical examiner said quickly, as he came to stand by Jackie's Jeep. "Because you may take credit for her discovery."

"I wouldn't do that."

"I know that, Jackie. But does she?"

"I guess not."

"Get home safe," the medical examiner commanded. Jackie did what she was told.

CHAPTER 7

It was late when Jackie finally returned home. Peter was asleep. At first Jackie thought she would go right to bed, but the long hot shower she had taken to relax her muscles had actually woken her up. As she walked through her living room in her nightshirt, Jackie decided to spend a few moments looking at the videotape Ral had given her.

Jackie didn't bother with the sound. She had heard Keith Monahan's spiel so many times now that she could recite it word for word along with him. Instead, this time Jackie blocked out all notice of the radio show host and his guest and started concentrating on the reaction shots of the audience.

As Jackie watched, she saw that what Cosmo had suggested to her was true. From the point where Keith started the show all eyes were trained onto the set. Jane Bellamy really did have several index cards that she was looking at, but it was also clear that she was looking up frequently over the tops of her reading glasses to see what was happening onstage.

Next Jackie caught a close-up of Cosmo Gordon. He held an envelope, presumably containing the text of his remarks, but from the time Keith Monahan started the show, his eyes too were glued to the screen. The same was true for Henry Obermaier. The big man was safely ensconced in the biggest and most luxurious of the guest chairs, giving the other guests a glimpse of the skewed priorities that ruled academia. Last to arrive, as advertised, was Alice Blue who, Jackie noticed, was looking off at something in the background. Jackie ran the tape back a couple of times to see if she could see what it was that the activist/homemaker was looking at.

No luck. The tape had been shot with Communications School equipment that was decidedly not in the best of condition. Jackie tried the pause, but on her VCR the lines of tracking static had obliterated precisely the areas Jackie wanted to examine.

Now determined to explore this mystery, despite the lateness of the hour, Jackie dragged her off-line recording machine in from her den and started fiddling with the various power cords. This was a task normally left for Peter but without a man around impatiently fussing or making fun of her, Jackie was able to figure it out on her own.

Now able to get a clean pause, Jackie brought her red, straw-filled hassock over to the television so close her nose was practically touching the screen. Jackie couldn't make out what Alice appeared to be looking at. There was a patch panel of some kind, a room, possibly a rest room or some sort of supply closet, and a couple of folding chairs set against the sound-resistant foam walls.

What could she have seen? Someone sitting or coming out of the room that she hadn't expected to see. A ray gun of some kind protruding from the patch panel? A gray-painted face sticking out of the soundproofing panels?

All of a sudden, there was a knock on her door.

"Hello?" Jackie called out.

"Jackie!" a loud nasal voice called out to her. "It's me. Xenia! I'm sorry to bother you so late but can I come in for a moment?"

Jackie groaned. It was Matt Dugan's widow, Xenia, who had moved in recently with her two small girls.

Although Jackie had all the sympathy in the world for the woman after her bereavement, she had found, in the short time that the Dugans had shared a duplex with her, that Xenia was a woman who believed her problems, whatever they may be, were meant to be shared with the world around her, as quickly as they came up.

"What's up, Xenia?" Jackie asked, opening the door but leaving the chain lock on.

"Oh, hello . . . Oof." Xenia crunched nearsightedly against the door. "Oh, what is it? Is there something wrong with your door? You know, the closet door in the girls' room squeaks too. Is there something you can do about that? I'm just helpless when it comes to mechanical things."

"I guess a little oil would be the answer, Xenia. You'll have to excuse me for not inviting you in. I have my video equipment spread all over and things are kind of a mess."

"Oh, I know how you single women are. Messy, messy, messy," Xenia smiled. A fairly attractive woman under the right circumstances, Xenia Dugan favored the no makeup, gym-suit look at home. "Oh, what am I talking about? I'm single now, aren't I? Oh."

"Yes, well, I'm sorry you're having troubles with your closets, Xenia, but as I've told you a few times now, I'm really not the super of this building, so if you'll excuse me."

"I know I'm terrible coming down here like this. Bothering you so late and all . . ."

Jackie nodded. So far she was in complete agreement.

"But how's a person supposed to cope without friends, you know. Especially when you've lost your husband in the line of duty."

Jackie nodded, waiting for the punch line. The first half-dozen times Xenia had opened a conversation with this gambit she had felt sorry for her. The problem was, Xenia, whether she realized it or not, was milking her widowhood for all it was worth. Xenia was not hurting for money, and it was as Jackie was telling Cosmo Gordon the other day (the medical examiner too had been initially very supportive of his friend's widow, then, after dozens of requests for favors, he had cooled considerably), it wasn't as if the couple had been torn apart by an assassin's bullets. After all, Matt and Xenia had been separated, and had all but filed the final divorce papers quite some time before the ex-policeman was shot down in an alley outside Leanna's Piano Parlor where the ex-cop worked a couple of days a week, breaking up shipping crates into firewood.

"I don't mean to be rude, Xenia," Jackie said quickly. "But I really do have a lot of work to do."

"Oh, but please, Jackie." Xenia pushed against the door again. Without her thick-lensed glasses Xenia was nearly blind. "Can't we just have a hot chocolate and talk for a while? I just can't sleep, lately. I've been watching reruns of that television show you used to write for, *CopLady*, and it reminds me of Matt."

Jackie wasn't sure she saw the connection, but decided it would be the height of foolishness to pursue the conversation. "Xenia, I'm really sorry. But it's like I told you last week. As much as I sympathize with you, I really am busy. Good night now."

Jackie shut the door. Despair washed over her. Even though Xenia had forfeited most of the sympathy she would have otherwise gotten by taking advantage of everyone who was willing to listen to her, Jackie still felt bad for her and knew she probably always would. Death was terrible enough, Jackie thought, and it was worse when it left so many piles of emotional debris.

A few moments after Xenia finally went back upstairs, Jackie settled back down to the videotape again. It was now harder for her than ever to make heads or tails of what was going on. Finally an idea came to her. Walking over to her desk, Jackie checked the syllabus and confirmed that David Surtees was teaching tomorrow. Surtees had recently returned from a hiatus in Europe working for the network covering the Olympics. Jackie more than suspected that if she approached the young film and video editor just right, she could get him to blow up that back wall and examine it with her.

Alice Blue thought she was going to solve this crime before her? Not a chance.

CHAPTER 8

The main auditorium was packed, as it always was whenever David Surtees gave one of his lectures. The thin, serious, former Jesuit scholar was not the best lecturer in the program. That honor would probably go to Ivor Quest or Fred Jackson. Surtees was, however, absolutely unique in that he told you things you did not know, and would not have seen without his help. David Surtees, in short, extended horizons—the job that all teachers are hired to do, but few ever actually accomplish.

Today the editing instructor was lecturing on the Zapruder film. "Today we study an amateur photographer's film," Surtees began as he stood nervously at a lectern wider across than he. "Ivor Quest should feature Abraham Zapruder in his Entertainment Entrepreneurs class because in terms of profit, Mr. Zapruder's first and only film cannot be topped either in audience recognizability factor or in cost to produce to profit ratio. For a total of about forty dollars and the happy accident of being at Dealey Plaza with a motion picture camera on the day John F. Kennedy was killed, Mr. Zapruder made more than a quarter of a million dollars."

Surtees waited for the amazed murmurs to quiet, then he resumed reading from his thick sheaf of notes. "The Zapruder film we know today, of course, has been edited. There are various speculations about who actually did the job. Some of the celebrity editors we have studied in this quarter are suspects.

"I don't imagine that we'll ever know for sure.

"The film has been edited in all the classic ways. It has been shortened, it has been optically enhanced, and it has been airbrushed. The illusion that is being presented to us in this film is that the President and his party were set upon by a lone gunman sniper as they whisked along in a publicity-oriented motorcade. That is the illusion. Here is how it was performed.

"Roll the video, please, Lang.

"Here is the famous shot of the motorcade coming down Dealey Plaza. Note here the overexposure in the opening frames. The editors considered using this overexposure throughout to wash out areas they didn't want you to notice. As you can see, this effect would not have worked because . . ."

Surtees pointed up at the top area left corner of the screen with a wooden pointer. "Here is the area supposedly overexposed . . ." The pointer then moved to the top right corner of the screen. "And here is the sun. How can the sun overexpose an area which is clearly in the shade when this area, clearly in bright sunlight, is not overexposed? They abandoned that trick as unusable."

Surtees paused a moment to let the murmurs die down and then resumed. "Here we see the President disappear behind the Stemmons Freeway sign.

"There are now three missing frames. There is much speculation as to what was on those three missing frames. People speculate about bullet holes appearing in the freeway sign and what not, which one can understand when one considers that the sign itself was rooted out of its concrete-based support poles and destroyed within hours of the assassination.

"Actually, I think what happened here was that Mr. Zapruder moved his camera to where he knew the President would emerge. If Mr. Zapruder's camera had clearly caught something he shouldn't have seen, in all likelihood the entire film would have been destroyed. Probably Mr. Zapruder along with it, if history is any judge."

Surtees paused to sip from a container of Goodwillie bottled water. "The missing frames supposedly lost in an accident by a careless technician, I believe, were used in the following ways. Pay attention."

Surtees resumed with the pointer. "Here we see the President's limousine moving forward. Assassination experts point out clearly where the President was shot in the back of the neck, where later the governor of Texas was shot, and then where the President was shot in the temple. There is no question, obviously, that there were any less than three shooters or that the shooters did not shoot from these angles here . . ."

Surtees then picked up a large wooden triangle and imposed it over the stilled frame to indicate the three points of a triangle. " . . . To achieve classic military triangulation." Surtees put the triangle back down.

"That is not the focus of our class today. What we will examine is what was done to the rest of the frame . . ." Surtees then resumed with the pointer. "Here and here.

"First we need a little background. Lang!" The Zapruder film faded out from the screen and the auditorium lights came back up. Surtees resumed his place at the lectern.

"You are all familiar, I hope, with the term 'letter-boxing.' Generally speaking, motion pictures, particularly those shot in the fifties, are done in a ratio of approximately 3:5. Simply speaking, it means the films were shot to be shown on a rectangular screen.

"When television became popular in the late fifties, it put pressure on filmmakers to adopt a new aspect that would more closely conform to a two-by-three screen. Filmmakers were told in no uncertain terms that if they did not make their films to conform with this new aspect,

then their films would not be purchased for television or
that when they were shown they would be butchered.

"You see at this time the motion picture business and
the television industry were at odds. The motion picture
tycoons, in order to offer the public something they
could not see at home for free, had to go to stunts, wide-
screen gimmicks like Todd AO Vision, Vista Vision, or
Cinerama; three and six color processes which gave you
more color than you could ever see on your color TV
even if you were one of the few hundred or so who had
one; 3-D and sillier gimmicks like Smell-O-Vision and
Percepto-Vision which consisted of a skeleton coming
out of the back wall of the theater and running over
your heads jingling its plastic bones during the climax
of a horror movie."

There was some scattered laughter and applause.

"I see we have some William Castle fans in the
audience. Try not to scare anyone. Anyway, TV was
financed by the same companies that had financed radio.
Deep-pocket companies like our own Falk & Goodwillie,
which at one time sponsored most of the soap operas
shown during the day. They tried to force the movie
people to drop their gimmicks; the most popular of
these being the wide screen, and eventually they won.
Their win had a cost, of course. And that was that the TV
screen they were going to show movies on, a TV screen
that could have just as easily been built in a rectangular
movie screen form, didn't show all the movie that was
running through its projectors.

"Early movie-on-TV showings were marked by de facto
overlap edits that left people playing love scenes with
other actors who weren't on camera. Cowboys shot
at off-screen Indians which left the audience at home
wondering if their bullet had found its target or not,
and so on. The independent unaffiliated television station
owner in a small market would just buy the eight- or
sixteen-millimeter prints shown at 4-H Clubs or Snooker

Halls and let them run as is. When films were bought, at great expense, by networks as product for their big advertiser-supported showcases such as *The Saturday Night Movie*, then the movie would be carefully panned and scanned.

"Painstakingly, scene by scene or in some cases even shot by shot, the best two-by-three slice would be transferred onto a new print. If Monument Valley in a John Ford film ended up looking like your local granite quarry, of if home audiences missed seeing Alfred Hitchcock make his cameo in *North by Northwest*, well what did you expect for free entertainment?

"People finally started catching on in the early eighties when Woody Allen refused to release his film *Manhattan* to video unless it was letterboxed.

"What does that have to do with the Zapruder film? Lang, turn us back on."

The lights dimmed again and Surtees resumed pointing with his pointer. "Look closely—a letterbox section of the Zapruder film is all that remains of the original. The top of the first frame here has been duplicated as you see and pasted onto the next four frames. Need proof? Look at the position of the tree here. The car is moving forward but the tree stays exactly the same distance away. Something is being covered up. Something is happening at the top half of the frame that somebody else doesn't want you to see. What, for instance?

"Let's look at this hair here, apparently a strand that just happened to blow onto the lens for three frames. Unusual, wouldn't you say, that a hair would land on the lens and stay there for only three frames? Even more unusual when we see that the hair does not distort the image as we see dust and hair and bits of fluff do in other films. No, here we can see a bit of a scene shot through the hair. Is there such a thing? A hair that flies on and off lenses and turns transparent at opportune moments? Not in my experience. What is the hair covering?

"Now let's look at these cracks. Cracks in the film it seems. Then why don't the cracks extend to the edges here? I have never seen a crack that started in the middle of a piece of film and didn't extend to the edges and I've been in the editing trade a long time. What happens when we do infrared analysis of those cracks?

"Lang." The image was replaced with its negative and red streaks became visible appearing from three separate directions.

"As you see, they become the tracers from bullets. High-powered projectiles leave a discernible bullet trail even in bright daylight. Where do the bullets come from?

"Lang!" The image went back to normal.

"This shadow here," Surtees pointed out.

Jackie leaned forward in her chair to see more closely, since this was precisely the sort of thing she was interested in.

"Covered with the hair. We remove the hair with a computer . . ."

The image was replaced by newly edited footage. " . . . And what do we get? The figure of a man with a rifle. Now let's check the tree, here—the tree that stays in the same relative position no matter how fast the car moves. This noble oak has a decoration on it. See?"

Another adjustment was made and an optical zoom brought that particular area of the screen up closer and into sharper focus. "This black device here. It's hard to see in this doctored Zapruder film, so let me show you one firsthand."

Surtees then took a black cardboard aiming aide, an item that looked a little like a gridded pear with a hole in the center out of a box and held it high so that everyone in the auditorium could see it.

"Marksmen use items like these as reference points. Usually it's hung between two targets and it gives you a vertical reference line that you're not going to find when you are shooting at a round bull's-eye target.

Film editors use items like these too. For instance we are always trying to get set designers to put ladders or stacks of flat objects like books in a scene. When you're cutting and filling and blowing up pieces of the frame to fill, you need a vertical reference point to keep the viewer's eye occupied."

The lights were brought back up to half, so that some of the students could more easily take notes.

"What else? Look at this piece of sidewalk. Fuzzed, see? Yet the sidewalk right next to it on either side is not. What does that mean? Jackie, do you want to help us out? You all know Jackie Walsh, students."

The students all turned toward Jackie and she gave a wry look to Surtees and thanked goodness that she had been paying attention. "I'd say the frame has been fuzzed because there is a crack or bullet pit in the sidewalk which couldn't possibly exist if we believe that only four bullets were fired from the Depository angle."

"*Muy bueno*," Surtees responded, "as they say in Barcelona. Or you bet your bottom dollar as we say here in Pretty Palmer, Jewel of the Midwest."

"Do you have any further questions of me, Mr. Surtees?" Jackie asked sweetly.

"No, Ms. Walsh. We'll find out how much you really know when you take next week's quiz. Now, back to this." Surtees winked at Jackie, then turned back to the screen.

"Now look at the Secret Service driver of the presidential limousine. Look at the set of his shoulders. The driver, the senior Secret Service man in Dallas, is surprisingly relaxed, wouldn't you say? Especially when he knows that routine precautions, such as putting the bulletproof bubble on the convertible and sweeping the surrounding buildings to make sure windows are closed and no one is hanging out on rooftops, haven't been done. Watch our friend slowly look back after the first shot as if to make sure the President has been hit. Now see, he resumes his relaxed position as if nothing has happened. Does this fit with the driver's testimony before the Warren Commission that he was speeding up the car as they came out of the hairpin turn? Of course not. Yet the film seems to bear him out. The car does seem to be speeding up after it passes the highway sign. Why? Because frames of the film were removed."

"Lang."

The lights came up and the film image once more disappeared from the screen. "Missing frames," Surtees resumed. "That's why some of the prints of old movies you see are jerky.

"At one time in the early 1930s there was an enormous underground network among collectors, some of whom were film editors or projectionists. They would take frames of film cut from a print and blow them up into eight-by-ten photographs or in some cases into posters. Some clever editors took single frames or sequences from films and edited them into smokers to make it appear that Jean Harlow or Cary Grant were exposing themselves or nude bathing or having sex with dark sexy strangers. After a print had gone through a few hands there were often so many frames missing, the film would run five minutes shorter."

Jackie looked at her watch and saw that if Surtees wrapped up soon, she'd have time to have lunch with him. Then, catching the young editing instructor's eye, she made a churning motion with her hands, indicating "go faster."

"So what did we see today?" Surtees asked, a little unnerved at having to speed up his lecture. "The Zapruder film, a piece of history used as evidence in two separate conspiracy investigations, has been tampered with. Distracting bits of dust and a hair were added to obscure shapes and figures, frames were deleted to make it appear that the presidential limousine was picking up speed when in fact it was slowing down. Bullet trails were made to appear as cracks in the film, airbrushing was used to remove a chip gouged out of the sidewalk, and a cut and paste hid the appearance of a sniper. This sort of thing, clumsily executed as you can see, is done every minute of every day. Here the editing was done to criminally tamper with evidence. For the most part editing is done just to present a story via sounds and pictures in a proscribed period of time. Other times editing is done to cover mistakes, acting, directing, or technical.

"Editing can also be used to slant a story. Obviously. It's why so many news programs now are having troubles with guests who want their interviews to run unedited or not at all.

"If your favorite cartoon characters have higher voices than you remember from when you were a child it's due in part to the fact that the videotapes these cartoons are shipped on are electronically condensed by their sellers so that they can show more commercials. If the background crowd of onlookers in most local TV news programs always seem to be the same group of people, it's because they've gotten tired of getting each new group of people to sign waivers. So they just edit in the same crowd shots every time. And so it goes, as the former film editor turned famous novelist once said.

"Editing is a challenge, its rewards or disappointments depend on how hard you are willing to work—or how creative you can force yourself to be. The editor in today's world can be just some manipulative hack or he can serve the way students of past fine arts great masters did.

"You know, painters like Titian or Rembrandt or Hals did not paint every inch of their giant canvases. They blocked out the painting, put in certain details with charcoal, and then painted the more difficult parts of the painting—the subjects' faces, a globe or curlicue that especially interested them.

"Many years ago, the papers of one of Cezanne's students was found. And in his sketchbook they found a yellowed clipping from George Bernard Shaw in his days as an art critic. Shaw had found the figures in Cezanne's painting stilted and uninteresting but he said in his review that he was particularly struck by the marigolds in the painting—obviously something this student had painted.

"The student died in obscurity, far less well off than his master, but he had the satisfaction of knowing as he died that at least once in his life, he was considered as great an artist as any painter who had ever lived."

The entire way to the Juniper Tavern, Jackie pressed compliments on Surtees for his lecture. He was embarrassed but did not denigrate his accomplishments, for that would have been dishonest.

They then entered the friendly portals of the burger and brew tavern run by Reg White, a bold-mustachioed expatriate Australian, who had resisted the Palmer and Midwest habit of naming his restaurant after himself because he found the idea of calling a place where people came to eat and drink after himself both sacrilegious and a wee bit cannibalistic.

"Did you miss the Juniper?" Jackie joked as they squeezed into one of the place's smoky, rickety old booths.

"More than I missed the Sturbinger cafeteria," Surtees quietly joked back.

"Honestly," Jackie responded. "I don't know how it lasted as long as it did. When people finally stopped complaining about the food and just refused to go there anymore, the university shut it down. I think they're going to put in one of those combo food chains with donuts and hot dogs and fried chicken and hamburgers."

"I vote for pizza myself," Surtees replied. "That's what I missed most in Barcelona."

"How was covering the Olympics?"

Surtees laughed again, louder this time. "You make it seem like I was gliding from event to event with a notebook in my hand collecting scoops like Charles Lane."

Jackie slapped the table in merriment. "I *loved* Charles Lane. Do you know he's still working? I remember him from silent films."

"Always with the fedora with a press card in the hatband," Surtees supplied.

"And whenever he would spot Claudette Colbert or Olivia De Havilland as the runaway heiress . . ."

" . . . Sneaking through town with the disreputable likes of Clark Gable or Robert Montgomery . . ." Surtees added.

"Lane would spot Bette Davis or someone, slumming in the railroad yard, push back the brim of his hat with his thumb and say . . ."

"Say . . . Aren't you . . . ?" Jackie and Surtees finished this together and then collapsed in great gales of laughter.

"Say," interrupted Reg White, right on cue, although he did not push back a hat on his head and the word came out more like "Sigh . . ."

Surtees and Jackie turned.

"Did anyone take your drink order yet?"

"No," a slightly dazed Surtees replied.

"We haven't actually been here very long," Jackie nodded. She knew that the service had been dicey at the Juniper since Rachel Gibson, the officiously "too nice" day waitress, had been fired for stealing from the till.

"What'll you have?" Reg asked.

"Well," Surtees replied, picking up a menu. "I'd like a lemonade. And can I order food?"

"If it's expensive enough," Reg joked, deadpan. "Don't tell me you're having just the plain beef sandwich which you want cooked in a time-consuming way."

"Worse than that, I'm afraid," Surtees replied. "I want a cheddar cheeseburger, bunless, cooked medium on the edges and medium well in the center with mustard and two toasted corn muffins on the side."

"Very good, sir. I'll toe dance out to the kitchen and get that for you." Reg pretended to snarl. "And for the madame? Some equally irritating dish with a big frosty glass of free ice water?"

"Well the ice water part sounds good," Jackie smiled. "And I'll have a cup of coffee to drink too. That's not too expensive although I notice that even though the coffee bean shortage crisis is over you haven't brought the price back down. And for lunch I think I'll have a thrifty smoked turkey sandwich with lettuce and tomato, mustard not mayonnaise, on whole wheat toast if you have it."

"If we don't, I'll send a boy on horseback to fetch it from the local grocery emporium," Reg assured her.

"And a Waldorf salad," Jackie concluded, handing Reg her menu.

The tavern owner clicked his heels and said, "Feel free to move to a table for six or eight if you're feeling cramped in this little four-person booth. Nothing's too good for our high-rolling prize customers."

Surtees laughed heartily as Reg stalked off with an intentionally silly walk. "He's a gasser, isn't he?"

"The best," Jackie confirmed. "Do you know where he got the name for this place?"

"Some old Australian TV show starring Paul Hogan?"

"Close," Jackie responded. "The Juniper Tavern was a legendary highwayman's tavern where the unwary stopped for a drink or a room and ended up getting their throats cut. Reg told us that since he intended opening a place where you had to pay three times as much for a hamburger beef sandwich as you would in any chain restaurant, he would do his best to warn people before they came in."

"That's priceless," Surtees agreed. "So? What are we talking about? Oh, you asked about Barcelona. Well, obviously an editor never gets to see much of anything. You sit in a video booth or a gloomy drip room where no matter how many fans they give · you, it's always too hot. You wear white gloves and look at the arms and legs of similarly built athletes all day. If you're experienced at this kind of nonsense, then they put you in charge of trying to figure out which leg or arm belongs to which contestant so the paint-box people can put their names and little national flags under their images as they finish up whatever event you had to wade through four hours of film of to find thirty usable seconds.

"You work at night, not so much because Barcelona's hot but because all of Spain functions on the evening to dawn schedule."

"Does that mean they sleep all day?" Jackie asked.

"No," Surtees responded. "They work or play till four or five, then get up at the same time we do. They put in a morning of work, then knock off for lunch and a siesta. Here in the States workers holler like a scalded coon if you want them to work a split shift. In Spain they consider you the blackest-hearted slave driver who ever lived if you propose anything but."

Jackie settled back comfortably in her seat. She liked hearing interesting stories about far-off climes. "So, did you do any sightseeing?"

"Some," Surtees conceded. "We had at least a couple of hours off during the day. The rest of the time we'd have to take turns in the video truck switching over feeds from one event or another for the special channels that offered the supposedly uninterrupted coverage although there were as many shots of talking heads in studios or doing interviews standing in front of phony-looking Spanish backgrounds as ever. And sooner or later you have to do the usual editor hat in hand shuffle . . ."

Reg White's fifteen-year-old daughter tiptoed over and laid down the drinks.

" . . . to the various cameramen and directors, begging them to get a shot or two that you needed for something or urging them to make your life a little easier by shooting a slate every once in a while with the numbers and if possible the faces of the competitors in each meet.

"You don't know how many times an on-cam airhead would interview someone's manager or former college luge instructor and never bother to get the person's full name and find out how it was spelled. Then we'd be there using our high school Spanish to try to get someone on the phone, then ask him in another language for the information. We had to scratch one of the best interviews because we never could ascertain whether 'Yul No Last Name' spelled his first name like Yul Brynner or Tom Ewell."

"Sounds horrible," Jackie commented.

"Oh, don't get that impression," Surtees replied, sipping his drink. "Like with most things you get so caught up in the silliness that you forget to mention the truly wonderful things. For instance, I almost didn't go to the bullring. You know—who wants to look at pointless cruelty when I can just go to Los Angeles? Anyway, just as I was about to blow the whole thing off I found out they had a variation I had to see—bullfighting in a swimming pool."

"What?"

"I kid you not," Surtees swore, solemnly putting his hand over his heart. "They have it in the corrida. The bulls are a little smaller than the big Pamplona fighting toros, and their horns are shaved down halfway and plastic-capped."

"But it still smarts real good when they gore you," Jackie surmised.

"It does indeed," Surtees confirmed. "The bull stands in a high-walled round swimming pool about twelve feet wide. There are 'Swimadors,' I don't know what they really call them, and the idea is this—you have to get into the pool and throw a little round plastic ring around one of their horns. You get a ringer, you win."

"I bet that's a lot tougher than it sounds."

"You'd win that bet," Surtees agreed. "That bull doesn't want to share its pool with you. And when you start tossing things at its head, that bull's first impulse is to take that ring and shove it down your throat. It's a lot of fun to watch though."

Jackie gave that one a dubious headshake. "You should have gotten a camera crew down there and put that on a videocast."

"No offense"—Surtees nodded, smiling as Reg's mute daughter, Ryan, served the plates of food—"but you're not even in the first hundred people to suggest that to me. We all begged them. We all pleaded with them. We even got them down to the ring and had them agree it was a darn good show. But their only response was that 'it's not an Olympic event so we won't show it.' If a flying saucer from Arcturus had appeared over the stadium and started dropping down giant killer robots with death-ray bazookas, the networks wouldn't have given them airtime on the basis that planetary invasions aren't a regularly scheduled Olympic event." All of a sudden Surtees stopped himself in midthought.

"What's the matter?" Jackie asked, afraid that he might have broken a tooth or swallowed a sliver of glass, or something.

"I was just thinking," Surtees replied. "One of the cameramen I dealt with there was killed by a sniper while riding in some closing ceremony procession."

"Oh, I'm sorry. Did you know . . . ?"

Surtees nodded. "One moment you're cursing some-one out for never getting clear shots of the numbers on the participants' backs, and the next moment you're attending his funeral."

There was a moment of silence, then Jackie said, "Well, this time is as good as any to bring up what I wanted to talk to you about today, David."

"What's that?" Surtees asked, snapping to and clearly grateful for the change of subject.

"You've heard that the police are now convinced that Mannheim Goodwillie was murdered?"

Surtees nodded.

"The scene of the crime . . ."

" '*Locus en quo*' the legal chappies say," Reg White offered as he refilled Jackie's cup in passing.

" . . . was sealed off," Jackie continued. "I could probably get permission to inspect the premises since I'm friendly with one of the homicide detectives."

"Lieutenant McGowan," Surtees supplied. Seeing Jackie's questioning look, Surtees explained, "I remember him from the Danielle Sherman investigation. Anyway, Dannie and I . . . we dated a couple of times, you know?"

"No, I didn't know," Jackie replied, giving Surtees a sympathetic look.

"Stuff happens. Anyway . . ."

"Ral Perrin taped the program they were doing when Mr. Goodwillie died," Jackie explained. "I've looked at the video and need help."

"You want to optically enhance certain areas of the frame?"

Jackie nodded. "That's part of it. It was what I was going to ask you before I heard your lecture. After hearing what you said about seeing tracer streaks from bullets . . ."

"You can't see those with the naked eye. You need an infrared viewer," Surtees quickly pointed out.

"Do you think," Jackie asked, "you could put the videotape through a special viewer and see what direction the microwaves were coming from?"

David leaned back thoughtfully in his chair. "I could try."

"That's all we're asking."

Surtees stroked his chin. "I'd need some clearance to use some special equipment in the Science department. Brooks's lab."

"Really, you work with John? That's great."

"Oh, you know him?"

"His wife Millie and I have been friends since high school," Jackie smiled.

"Who says Palmer's not a small town?"

"Not me. Anyway," Jackie continued, "I'm going to try to schedule an interview with Dean Foreman this afternoon. I'll get his permission."

Surtees gave Jackie a narrow look. "I'm letting myself in for an awful lot of work if I do this."

Jackie picked up the meal check and gave the young editor her most winning smile. "Lunch is on me then . . ."

Surtees laughed and stuck out his hand. "You've got yourself a deal."

Jackie could not believe that after finally getting rid of the dragon of the Communications department, she now had to deal with her all over again.

Polly Merton, who both dressed and acted like a mean nun, almost smirked when Jackie walked into the chairman's office of the English department. Unfortunately for Jackie, the acting president of Rodgers University, Algernon Foreman, was Polly Merton's new boss.

"Hello, Polly!" Jackie said, trying to sound cheerful and knowing full well that she wasn't fooling anyone.

Polly brushed a microscopic piece of lint from one of the long sleeves of her white polyester dress, then

pretended to look up and see Jackie for the first time.
"Yes? May I help you?"

Jackie bit her tongue before saying, "Over your dead
body," and instead answered, "I wonder if I may speak
to Dean Foreman for a moment?"

Polly gave Jackie her usual cold look-over, then pretended to consult her desk calendar. "Do you have an
appointment with President Foreman, Miz . . . ?"

"Walsh," Jackie supplied, grimly going along with
Polly's game. "No, I'm afraid I don't."

"Well, then," Polly replied, firmly closing her book.

"Would it be possible to have just a few words with
him on an unscheduled basis?"

Polly made a *tsk* sound that contained an entire year's
worth of derision. "*President* Foreman is very busy at
present, overseeing both the English department and
the affairs of the entire college. Obviously he does not
have time for everyone who just drops in to waste his
time."

Jackie felt the back of her neck burning. She thought,
not for the first time, that Polly Merton should make
special appearances at low blood pressure clinics. Five
moments alone with her would be all it would take.

"I certainly am not interested in wasting Dean Foreman's time," Jackie responded. "I have been asked to
help with the investigation of the unfortunate death of
Mr. Mannheim Goodwillie at the opening of the Radio
Arts Building last week and . . ."

Polly pretended not to understand. "You were asked
by *President* Foreman?"

"No," Jackie replied, struggling to keep her temper.
"I was asked by Ivor Quest, but I need Dean Foreman's
permission to . . ."

"Ivor Quest . . ." Polly Merton repeated, as if struggling to recall the name. Of course the last time she
had talked to the great director he had told her to clean
out her desk. "I believe he is in the Communications

department." Polly took a half-size blue looseleaf College Directory from the shelf behind her. "Yes," Polly
confirmed, slowly finding the listing. "He is. I believe
his new secretary is Ms. Zweiback. Poor woman. That's
such a terrible place to work. So many hysterics running
around making impossible demands. Do you want her
number? I'll write it down on this card."

"Ms. Merton," Jackie said tightly. "Let's stop this
nonsense, shall we? May I leave a note for President
Foreman."

Polly gave a small smile of triumph having finally
gotten Jackie to refer to her boss as "President." "Not
with me. *Dean* Foreman hates little notes. He's been
very clear on that point."

Jackie knew that Foreman had probably told Polly,
an inveterate writer of little notes, that he didn't want
her to leave him any more notes. And of course, the
irritating department secretary, as usual, was interpreting
her boss's orders in a way most convenient to herself.
"May I make an appointment then?"

"Certainly. Let's see." Polly opened the appointment
calendar book again. "Dean Foreman has some time
available for a brief chat, on the seventeenth of next
month."

Exasperated, Jackie turned and walked away.

Still fuming, Jackie was almost to the side door of
Armstrong Hall when she was hailed from an open
cubicle.

"Jackie!"

Jackie turned to see Paul Cook, a thin, bearded, long-
faced teacher of Portuguese literature.

"Oh, hi, Paul," she responded.

"Paolo," he corrected her. "I'm going totally Portuguese."

"Okay," Jackie responded, a little taken aback. "How're
Sara and Isaac?"

"Fine, fine. You forgot to ask about our adopted son, Peter." Paolo said the last with a sardonic grin to let her know he wasn't serious.

"Uh-oh. Peter becoming a little ubiquitous for you?"

"No, not at all," Paolo reassured her. "It's just that we don't see enough of his mother. I don't remember the last time you came over to show us your deadly lawn dart technique. What's the matter? Your Lieutenant Columbo boyfriend taking up all your free time?"

"Free time? You'll have to get me a dictionary. I'm not sure I know the meaning of the phrase," Jackie replied. "What about you? Read any good epic poems lately?"

"As a matter of fact, I have. Come in for a moment, will you? I've got something to show you."

Jackie gave her friend a suspicious look, but figured he was a good guy and if this was just a practical joke of some kind, it wouldn't be too awful a one.

As Jackie walked into the colorful office with its *El Cid* posters and serapes and replica pre-Columbian figurines scattered about, she said, "Is it real important, Pau . . . Paolo? I'm kind of on the run."

Paolo walked slowly to his desk and Jackie turned and saw there was someone else in the room, a hunched-over butterball of a man. Somewhere in his early seventies, Algernon Foreman, the department chairman, the acting president of the largest single-site university in the United States, looked like a scared rabbit. "Hello, Miz Walsh."

"Dean Foreman!" Jackie said in some surprise.

"Shhh!" Paolo Cook said at once.

"The walls have ears you know," Foreman added.

Jackie restrained a slight impulse to laugh. Down in the dumps like this, Algernon Foreman sounded a little bit like the cartoon character Droopy.

"What are you doing here?" she asked.

"Hiding"—Foreman gave a sideways twitch of the head—"from her."

"Ms. Merton," Jackie guessed at once.

Foreman's head nodded jerkily. "She's like an evil Mother Teresa."

"She takes some getting used to," Jackie smiled.

"This is no laughing matter," Foreman replied gloomily. "That woman has got the entire department terrorized. My Chaucer instructor said she almost killed her today. Bawled me out something terrible. Told me if I didn't get rid of that woman she was quitting at the end of the term. She and half the department. She was so upset she was yelling at me in Olde English. Barely understood what she was saying."

"Well," Jackie said placatingly, "at least your files are in a little better shape now."

"Well, fiddle dee dee. My files were in good enough shape before," Foreman whined. "I don't care what other people thought. I liked the old system. That's why I kept it for so many years. If the girls couldn't find a memo and had to get up and go through a few cardboard boxes, what did it matter? There was no rush. Most of the writers we teach have been dead hundreds of years. I liked watching the girls bend over. Kept me young."

After a long moment, Paolo poured the dean a bracer of Madeira from a hanging wine sack. Jackie sat in the visitor's chair.

Foreman threw down the drink in a gulp. "Thank God for Paolo here."

Paolo pointed to what looked like a ventilation panel on the wall, and twisted a knob on it. Jackie could then hear Polly Merton pecking away at her word processor while relentlessly humming Grieg's *Sorcerer's Apprentice* under her breath.

"What's she doing?" Foreman asked. "Putting bits of tape on paper clips again? I couldn't believe it. I called her in and said, 'Answer me, Nurse Wretched. Why

are you taping my paper clips? They don't hold paper
as well.' She said she was coding them for 'sorting pur-
poses.' 'Coding?' I said. 'There's only two sizes. What's
so hard about that? You put the little ones in one bowl
and the big ones in another bowl. If a couple of them
end up in the wrong bowl, it's not such a tragedy.' Well,
I don't have to tell you, it's like shouting down a well.
She says, 'They're not coded for size, they're coded by
arrival date. This way,' she tells me, 'we'll use up all
the old ones first.' Can you believe it? Freshness dating
for a bunch of little pieces of folded tin guaranteed to
last four hundred years."

"Uh, Dean Foreman," Paolo interrupted, "you might
want to try to bring your voice down a little."

A fear-ridden Foreman immediately clapped both
hands over his mouth.

"I know she can be a terror," Jackie responded.

"Dean Foreman is trying to get her moved over to the
president's office and have her set up shop there," Paolo
explained.

"Then you can bet," Dean Foreman assured all and
sundry, "I won't go within fifty yards of the place."

Jackie and Paolo exchanged secret smiles.

"And there's little doubt that I won't palm her off on
whatever poor sap they appoint to replace me." Foreman
held out his empty glass and Paolo rushed to refill it.

Jackie used the opportunity to come to the point. "Uh,
Dean Foreman. I know you don't want to attract any
unnecessary attention, so I'll tell you what I need and
tiptoe out."

"Time was," Foreman reminisced, "when a fellow
could sit of an afternoon and contemplate great literature. Cuddle up with a fat volume of Colin Wilson and
recharge the lymph nodes. Not with that woman around.
Has one scheduled like a Mussolini train conductor. I've
had to talk to so many people I've got opera tenor's
laryngitis."

"You might know, President Foreman," Jackie continued, undaunted, "that I've been interviewing several people on their impressions of the Mannheim Goodwillie killing."

"Manny's moldering in the ground," Foreman moped. "I almost envy the man."

"Now, now," Paolo comforted the dean. He poured Foreman another half glass of Madeira. Before he could raise the spout, however, Foreman's liver-spotted left hand snaked out and pushed it back down to fill the glass.

"Anyway, Dean Foreman."

"Yes, yes, Ms. Walsh, the investigating." Foreman transferred the glass into his other hand so he could shake off drops of wine. "Let me tell you, if you haven't been told before, how grateful the college is for your help with this second dreadful murder matter. Although"—Foreman raised his drink to his lips and took a thoughtful sip—"one's current station makes one wonder if those Free Merida women aren't correct after all. Maybe Phil Barger really did kill himself. That old bat out there would drive you to spray a shopping mall full of people with an automatic weapon."

"Calm down, Dean Foreman," Paolo urged.

"Hah," Foreman replied in a maudlin voice. "I hold out my arms and welcome Death's icy embrace."

"What I wanted to ask you, Dean Foreman," Jackie started again.

"It's not just me, you know," Foreman insisted. "There isn't a chairman in the college that would have her. Your boss, Ivor Quest, told the board flat out that he wouldn't take the job if they didn't transfer her out. They looked down their list. Found that I was on vacation and moved like ninjas in the night."

"Dean Foreman . . ."

"Yes, yes?" Foreman shook his wobbly head. "You'll have to excuse me, Ms. Walsh. I vowed to drink myself insensible this afternoon and as you can see, I'm almost there."

"All I need from you," Jackie said quickly, "is permission to have David Surtees use some college equipment in the Science department to enhance a video that was taken at the time Mannheim Goodwillie was killed."

Foreman waved his hand stupidly. "Anything, anything. Paolo?"

"You've still got some, sir."

"Not for long," Foreman said quickly. "But first, take this down on paper, will you?"

Paolo smiled and reached for a memo pad.

" 'Let it be known I have appointed the bearer of this note, Ms. Walsh, as special vice president.' " Foreman turned and shot Jackie a drunken wink. "And don't let this appointment affect your spelling."

He then turned to Paolo. "Let her do as she will. Signed Algernon Foreman, President Under Protest."

"Really, Dean Foreman." Jackie broke into laughter.

"He's serious," Paolo smiled.

"It's a nothing title, Ms. Walsh, I assure you." Foreman wiped his lips with his handkerchief. "It means you will be my special investigator. Like that chap in those wonderful adventure books, *Ed Noon, Secret Agent to the President*. You won't get an office or a pay raise. You'll have to keep teaching those awful film students. If you play your cards right, however, I might be able to swing you some stationery."

Paolo took the note to Jackie and shook her hand. "Congratulations, Special Vice President."

"Now," Foreman's depressed voice was heard again. "You're a heartbeat away from misery."

"Uh, thank you." Jackie's head whirled. "Would either of you know, by any chance, how I could get ahold of Henry Obermaier? I've been trying him for several days and he hasn't returned my calls."

"I'm having a party this evening," Foreman replied. "For our new best-selling authoress, that film director, what's her name? Ah, yes, Georgiana Bowman. A great catch for the University Press, Ms. Walsh, thanks to you."

"Thanks to Celestine Barger, you mean." Jackie had been tapped by the legendary pioneer film director to collaborate with her on her autobiography. Unfortunately, Jackie had been so exhausted by participating in her most recent murder investigation that she had been forced to recommend her friend Celestine instead. The college and the two collaborators had done very well by the book. Although put out by the small university press as a trade paperback, the book was a big hit and already in its third printing.

"Whatever." Foreman waved his hand negligently again and nearly fell over.

"I'd love to come, sir," Jackie prevaricated. "But our lengthy little chat, as productive and as informative as it was . . ."

"Come to the point!" After a brace of drinks Foreman's strain of Goodwillie blood (he was Stuart and Mannheim's first cousin) came out.

Jackie came to the point. "I really do have to find Henry Obermaier and talk to him before he leaves."

"Another fellow who despises that woman, you know?" Foreman informed Jackie. "That frog Hupfelt and one of his men had to physically restrain President Obermaier from backhanding her once."

Foreman's words reminded Jackie. She would have to talk to the man who was supposedly keeping the VIP guest comfortable, College Security Chief Walter Hupfelt.

"Anyway," Foreman continued, "Obermaier will be there tonight."

"Oh, he will?" Jackie asked.

"I may be seeing double, but I don't have to repeat things, do I?" Foreman was becoming positively waspish. "Come at eight. Costumes are optional. Do you know where I am? 137 Chestnut, near Ward Clement Drive."

"I'm sure I can find it."

"Bring your dog if you like."

"Really?" Jackie said in some surprise. "I can bring Jake?"

"What?"

"My dog's name is Jake."

"Oh, you really have a dog? Isn't that nice? I was joking actually." Dean Foreman explained ponderously, "I . . . I was making a reference to the fact that if you couldn't find the house you could bring a seeing-eye dog or a guide dog or . . . you know, I think I'm going to be sick."

As Paolo helped Foreman to his sink, Jackie beat a hasty retreat.

The game, she decided, was now very definitely afoot.

CHAPTER 9

"You know, you're never at home," Peter yelled at Jackie as she and her towel disappeared into the backyard.

"I know," Jackie replied. "It's your music. It drives me from the house."

"Yeah," Peter yelled after her, holding up with one hand the pants he hadn't gotten around to buckling. "Maybe that's why I'm becoming a delinquent!"

"You're not a delinquent, Peter!" Jackie yelled as she reached the end of her property and opened the fence to the Palmer Steel Recreation Project. "You're an underachiever! You've got to have some get-up-and-go to be a delinquent. Some of those hubcaps are on kind of tight."

Peter contemplated running after his mother and driving her to tears with his rapier rejoinders. After a moment, however, he decided to blow the whole thing off.

Jackie rinsed off under the outdoor shower, made Jake do the same, then mistress and dog raced to be the first one to dive into the public pool.

Jackie loved to swim and was glad that the city, confident that Stuart Goodwillie would reimburse them for it, had turned part of the abandoned Palmer Regular Steel Works into a municipal pool. Now, instead of having to go all the way over to the university and walk the entire length of the campus to use the College Field House's pool, all she had to do, practically, was go out in her backyard.

"Dive, Jake!" Jackie challenged her dog. A diver for the canine section of the Palmer police department, Jake could both dive deeper and hold his breath longer than his mistress. Jackie was making him work for it, though. She had already increased her lung capacity five or ten percent since she had started working out with Jake.

It should be stated, by the way, that Jackie was not doing anything in the least bit unorthodox. A half-dozen dogs accompanied their owners to the pool for a swim. Bonnie Greenstein, activist head of the City Council, was always alert to the sensitivity of special interest groups and Thalia Gilmore's Canine Rights Lobby had proven quite conclusively that dogs are cleaner than most humans.

Needless to say, outgoing Mayor Big Bill Curtis had shown his true colors once again by proclaiming snidely that maybe if certain low-class individuals would make a little more of an effort at basic hygiene, then that wouldn't be the case. But Jackie cared nothing for that. She just wanted to relax a while and romp with her dog.

On top of the party tonight, Jackie had a rehearsal of the benefit show for Keith Monahan. Fortunately, if the Foreman party didn't really get going until nine o'clock as Paolo and Sara Cook had assured her, then she could attend the rehearsal knowing that Henry Obermaier would still be there when she arrived.

After a good splash, Jackie went back to the house leaving Jake to give himself a lusty shake in her backyard.

Peter had been picked up by his father and although Jackie had teased her son before, she now felt a pang of sorrow. Jackie knew that her ex-husband Cooper, a salesman who still lived in the Palmer suburb of Kingswood, would never try to keep Peter full-time. The schedule that had developed the last couple of years since Jackie

and Cooper had broken up had suited her husband only
too well. More than two or three days with Peter every
two weeks and both father and son were miserable. Still,
Jackie didn't like her son to be out of the house for days
at a time. She knew it would be only too soon before he
was off to college and then she would be alone.

Jackie could have gone on with such thoughts indefi-
nitely, but then the phone rang. Diving for it, Jackie said,
"Hello?"

"Jackie Walsh?" an unfamiliar voice asked.

"Yes?"

"This is Sergeant Cornelius Mitchell of the Palmer
police department."

"Oh, Sergeant Mitchell. How are you?"

"Fine. Con's fine too."

"Good," Jackie smiled. "I'm Jackie."

"Well, Jackie. We've been grilling your mother's
canine burglar with a rubber truncheon."

"Oh, no. Not really?"

"No, I am kidding. If anyone ever got a video of three
policemen beating up a dog, there would be a conviction,
believe me. Can you come down to the station sometime
and we'll talk about what we've found out?"

"Sure. That would be great." Jackie fumbled her organ-
izer out of her purse and gave it a quick look. "Tomorrow.
Late afternoon."

"That's fine with me. I'm here till seven. Central
Precinct. Down in the basement all the way in the back.
Just follow the signs or follow your nose."

"All right, Con," Jackie laughed. "See you tomorrow."

Checking her olive-green blouse and tan pants outfit
in the mirror, Jackie added a hammered silver Mexican
necklace to the ensemble and then dashed for the door.

Paolo and Sara were waiting when Jackie pulled up
in her red Jeep. Jackie opened the passenger side door

so Jake could hop out, then took the old towel that Jake habitually sat on, shook it out, and stuffed it under the backseat.

"Sorry about the dog hair!" she yelled.

"That's quite all right," Sara replied, walking up to the Jeep while Paolo took Jake inside. "Remember, we've got three dogs ourselves, so we're used to it."

Jackie smiled, happy to see her friend. Although they were the same age, Jackie thought Sara had an older, more motherly disposition. A soft-sculpture artist who worked at home, Sara loved to cook and sew and mind children. It was unusual these days.

"You look very professional," Sara smiled, giving Jackie a warm hug.

"And you look very artistic," Jackie replied, referring to Sara's turban and embroidered frock.

"I look like Elizabeth Taylor in one of those awful sixties movies."

"Not at all," Jackie replied warmly. "Not until you get the violet contacts, anyway."

The two women shared a laugh and then Paolo came out of the house. "Sorry to keep you," he yelled, locking the front door. "Isaac's playing Tetris so I put Jake and the Doggie Andrews Sisters out back."

"I really appreciate Isaac volunteering to keep Jake company," Jackie replied. "Dean Foreman said we could bring him tonight, but I can't see that being appropriate."

Paolo laughed. "That's the thing about the Literature department parties. Anything and everything goes. I'll take the backseat."

"You sure?" Jackie asked, watched the tall, thin professor fold himself into the backseat.

"Positive," Paolo replied. "You two catch up. I'll snooze for ten minutes."

Sara and Jackie got in and buckled their seat belts. Jackie checked out the sprawled man in the backseat, then turned to her friend. "Can he really fall asleep back there?"

"Paolo can sleep anywhere," Sara assured their designated driver. "On our honeymoon he fell asleep on a tandem bicycle."

"Well, it was your honeymoon," Jackie protested.

Sara gave her a look. "It wasn't *that* exciting, Jackie—we had been living together for three years. He not only looks like an old hound dog, he can even sleep on top of a doghouse. Just like Snoopy, right, dear?"

"I prefer to think of myself as Dagwood," Paolo replied sleepily. "But with three dogs you never get a chance to snooze on the couch."

"Just don't go filling up on a foot-long sandwich," Sara responded.

"Pardon my snores."

Jackie smiled and touched Sara's knee. "It's good to see you, Sara."

"Ditto, stranger." Sara smiled, putting her hand over Jackie's briefly. "What's all this about you becoming embroiled in another murder investigation?"

"Sad but true, unfortunately," Jackie replied. "You know, the first couple of times it was kind of exciting. Now it's become a real pain in the neck."

Jackie dropped the Cooks off at Dean Foreman's house. They were going to set up for the party. With the Cooks not having a car, Jackie was always happy to exchange a little chauffeuring for all the times Sara and Paolo had invited Peter over for dinner or to spend the night.

"See you later," Jackie called as she brought the Jeep to a screeching halt before Dean Foreman's pleasant old clapboard house.

"If you don't see me," Sara replied. "Look in the kitchen. Come on, Paolo!"

Jackie had been told by Sara more than once that the bachelor Dean had a nasty habit of using his faculty and their spouses as unpaid domestic help. It was all done in a very jolly way. Dean Foreman would keep the drinks flowing and the praise fulsome, but at the end of the evening it amounted to the same thing. Many an English teacher went home utterly exhausted from what was supposed to be a relaxing evening.

The moment the Cooks moved away from the car, Jackie floored the gas pedal and sped off to Celestine Barger's house for the radio benefit show rehearsal.

As she feared, she was the last to arrive.

Celestine Barger, a small cheerful woman who more than a little resembled the late Gracie Allen, met her in the foyer of her gorgeously appointed ranch house and gave her a big Hollywood kiss on the cheek. "Jackie, how are you?"

"Frazzled," Jackie complained, looking at her hair in the hall mirror to see if the top had flattened out. "How are you, Ceil? Sorry I couldn't get here earlier."

"Don't worry," Celestine replied. "I was prepared. You told me, remember? And actually it's been rather fun to get up chairs and put out drinks and scripts for everyone. I haven't done that since *Triumphant Spirit*, don't tell me you don't remember?"

"Only you, me, and Cleveland Amory remember that one, Ceil."

"Still," Celestine turned on her friend with a familiar plaint, "we might have been the Kaufman and Hart of situation comedy, if you hadn't walked out."

"Walk out?" Jackie replied with familiar indignation. "We were fired, Ceil. Remember? I was pregnant, you had just gotten married. They told us to go to the library to look up some information on Henry Wallace and when we got back to the studio, the guard wouldn't let us in 'because we no longer worked there.' Then they brought out a handcart with all our possessions which they stuffed into a couple of bottled water boxes."

"All right," Celestine conceded, "so you didn't walk out, exactly."

Jackie grabbed Ceil by the shoulders and gave her friend a little shake. "I'm fine. You're fine. We made the right choices, okay? Did I hear someone say something about drinks?"

"Just call me Miss Kitty," Celestine responded. "What are you drinking?"

Jackie smacked her lips a couple of times experimentally. "You know what sounds good to me? White wine and Fresca."

"Gah," Celestine voiced her disapproval. "Well, let's see what I've got."

As Jackie followed her friend's decorous sojourn on three-inch heels through the house to the living room, she looked thoughtfully at the wall Celestine had devoted to photos and publicity. There they were. *Triumphant Spirit*, the marvelous sophisticated reworking of *Topper* that Jackie and Celestine had worked on. The networks had decided to cast the late Junior Samples in the role originally played by Leo G. Carroll with predictable results.

Then came *CopLady*. The second show had been a great deal more successful, running almost eleven years and launching more than a few careers. Jackie still got a residual check every once in a while from that one, but *Triumphant Spirit* really had a bigger piece of her heart. There were rumors, Jackie had heard, that the network was thinking of doing a *CopLady* reunion show. Jackie wondered, as she tore herself away from the memory wall and walked toward the dining room, what she would do if they called and offered her the chance to write it. Would she go to Los Angeles for a few months and make some money? Peter could come on weekends and then spend the summer with her. Hmm. It was a possibility anyway.

Jackie's reverie was interrupted by the booming voice of Fred Jackson. "Ho! Here comes the dummy. Now we can play bridge!"

"Fred!" Celestine said at once.

"Can't a man have a drink and be a little bit merry?"

"Not if 'merry' is to be used interchangeably with 'ass.' "

Fred frowned deeply. He hated women who had been educated in England.

"Pick up your scripts, everyone!" Celestine then ordered. "Frances, move that bottle out of Fred's reach. All right. Everyone knows Jackie. Jackie, you know everyone. As soon as you're ready, dear, we'll begin."

"I just need a drink of some kind . . ." Jackie replied.

Ronald Dunn, the handsome fiftyish former television spy and current supporting actor in films, jumped to his feet and flashed Jackie his twisted million-dollar smile. "Since you're the producer and we're all mere lackeys, let me do the honors, Ms. Walsh. What's your drink again? Fresca and white wine?"

Jackie nodded. She remembered her evening alone with the handsome, dark-haired former matinee idol and grew slightly weak-kneed.

"Here you are," Dunn said as he slipped the glass into her hand in a way that made Jackie blush. "My, don't you look lovely for a reading? I can hardly wait to see the performance ensemble."

Jackie, on the spot, considered blowing off the next day's interviews to go dress shopping.

"At the risk of ruining your evening," Dunn cooed in a thrilling low voice, "would you mind if I tell you how much I love this script?"

Dunn looked so sincere Jackie thought she might cry.

"I've read thousands of radio scripts in my research on my one-man Benny Show," Dunn continued. "And this is easily the funniest script on the page I have ever read. I'm terribly sorry. I really am. It's just, well . . . I just had to tell you that."

"Think nothing of it," Jackie breathed.

"Jackie!" Celestine called over to her. "Do you want your script, dear?"

"Sure."

Celestine stuck the script between the faces of the couple, breaking the spell. Dunn gave Jackie a warm smile, then walked back to his seat.

"Are you all right, Jackie?" Celestine asked with mock solicitousness.

"Mmm."

"Isn't it wonderful that you and our leading man manage to get along?"

"Wonderful."

"Are you sure you're going to be able to make it through our little rehearsal without a cold shower?"

"Let's begin!" Fred shouted, and Jackie regained her composure.

Sipping her drink, she opened her script and launched into the first speech. She was playing the part of the narrator/announcer. "Hello. Welcome to this evening's special broadcast of the *Golden Biscuit Good Radio Hour.* I'm Jackie Walsh, your host for the evening. Keith Monahan is in jail for a crime he didn't commit. Tonight's broadcast is dedicated to a man who was known as 'The King of Radio.' Remember—"

Marcus Baghorn, looking tanned and rested, responded with, "Your money or your life!"

Marcus had insisted on cutting his honeymoon short so he could come back and perform his semifamous Mel Blanc imitation.

Jackie continued, "There was a twenty-second pause— and that's a long, long time on radio, then—"

"Quit stalling. I said, your money or your life."

Ronald Dunn finally responded in a perfect Jack Benny, "I'm thinking it over!"

"For thirty years," Jackie continued, "Jack Benny was the biggest thing on radio."

"We'll hear thirty seconds of a scratchy version of *Love in Bloom* here, " Celestine interjected. She was keeping the others up on sound and special effects cues. "Then—"

"No, no, no," Marcus cried nasally in a Pepe Le Pew accent, once removed.

"Professor LeBlanc," Dunn/Benny said in his turn, "do you think you can ever make a good violinist out of me?"

"I do not know," Baghorn/LeBlanc replied. "How old are you?"

"Why?" asked Dunn/Benny.

"How much time do we have left?!"

"For another thirty years," Jackie continued, "Jack Benny dominated television."

Frances Costello raised her head and said as Mary Livingston would have, "Jack, why don't you stop being so stingy?"

"Mary," Dunn/Benny yelled. "I am not stingy, and you know it!"

"Oh, yeah?" Frances/Mary replied loudly. "Last year when you had to have your appendix out, remember how you wanted to let Rochester do it?"

"I did not!" Dunn/Benny replied, outraged. "I merely asked him if he knew how."

"Benny was also successful," Jackie continued, "with his live act, *An Hour and Sixty Minutes With Jack Benny*, and a half-dozen Hollywood films. It was on radio, however, that he really shone."

"Rochester!" Dunn/Benny shouted. "Oh, there you are."

Ral Perrin, pulling at his throat to make his voice raspy, said, "Yes, sir, Mr. Benny?"

"Where were you? Taking a nap? I've been looking all over for you."

"Sorry, Mr. Benny," Ral/Rochester replied. "I guess I am kind of tired. You know, I don't rest so good. I've been sleepwalking."

"Really? I didn't know."

"Oh, come now, Mr. Benny. I woke up one time and someone had put a vacuum cleaner in my hand."

"Benny's handpicked supporting cast," Jackie continued, "enhanced the prestige and success of their employer."

Mark Freeman then revealed his hitherto unappreciated tenor voice. As he did the big finish of "Mother Machree," some of the other readers burst into applause.

"And we'll have a tape here," Celestine explained, "and there will be riotous applause."

"Very good, Dennis!" Ronald Dunn did his next line. "Dennis Day, ladies and gentlemen!"

"The applause goes on obscenely," Celestine continued.

"Gee, they seem to like me, Mr. Benny," Mark/Dennis remarked innocently.

"Never mind that," hissed Dunn/Benny. "Get off the stage. Thank you, ladies and gentlemen. Thank you. Thank you. Hey, how about saving some of that for me?"

Jackie continued, "From Phil Harris . . ."

Dean Vingori of the Music department launched into a very credible Phil Harris, first singing a few bars, then greeting Dunn/Benny with, "Hey, Jackson. Still cutting your own hair, I see?"

"Riotous applause," Celestine explained.

"Ha, ha. Wonderful," the ersatz Harris responded, "truly wonderful. Oh, and you too, folks."

"To frequent guests," Jackie continued, "like Mr. and Mrs. Ronald Colman, 'who lived right next door.' "

"Well," said Ivor Quest, doing an impeccable Ronald Colman. "The cocktails are ready. A toast! Benita, your health!"

"Darling!" Frances supplied the stuffy Benita Hume Colman's voice.

"There's a tinkle of glasses," Celestine explained.

"Wellington!" Quest/Colman saluted again. "Champions salute champions. Happy days!"

"Tinkle of glasses."

"Benny," Quest/Colman said loudly. "We've had our differences, due to your unspeakably loutish American behavior. But let's bury the old cricket bat, shall we? Good health!"

"There is a loud sound of glass tinkling," Celestine explained. "Then a horrible breaking noise."

"Whoops!" Dunn/Benny exclaimed. "Too hard . . . I'm sorry. I didn't mean to break your glass."

"Oh," Frances/Benita replied sadly. "And that set was one hundred and fifty years old."

"Well, good," Dunn/Benny replied. "I'm glad I didn't break any of your new stuff."

Jackie followed quickly on Dunn/Benny's laugh line with, "Jack broke in against formidable competition."

Phil Watts, a man in his fifties with a toothbrush mustache, thick gray hair, and a stagily handsome face, was next to offer his contribution. Jackie had met Phil at a dog show and upon finding out that he was a gifted community theater actor, invited him to the benefit show to do his inimitable impression of Jack Pearl.

"Vass you dere, Sharlie?"

"But the Baron," Jackie narrated, "soon went down in flames. CBS sent in another vaudeville hall of famer with a comedy staff hired away from Benny."

"Hey," said Marcus Baghorn in a Joe Penner voice, "wanna buy a duck?"

"Joe Penner suffered the same fate as the Baron Munchausen," Jackie continued. "The other network then played its ace. Edgar Bergen and Charley McCarthy were moved to Sunday night opposite Jack Benny and in their first programs featured W. C. Fields as a recurring guest star."

"Look, Dad," Mark Freeman piped up woodily, "I can see the red light of the traffic signal from here."

"Now stop that, Charley," Ronald Dunn replied, easily lapsing into the part of Edgar Bergen. "You know very well that that is Mr. Fields's nose."

"Greetings, winesap," snarled the handsome magician Bill Reigert of "Bill and Lil, TWIN Magicians." "And as to you, kindling wood, watch your tongue or I'll set you ablaze with this ignitious cigar."

"Eventually," Jackie resumed, "CBS utterly conceded the spot to Benny."

"Hello, everyone. My name is Jack Benny. I will now pause fifteen seconds while everybody says, 'Who cares?' "

"Some guests with us tonight," Jackie continued, "recall Jack Benny's Hollywood career. Let's hear what Ivor Quest, Academy Award–winning director, has to say."

"He wasn't at all bad," Quest began.

"I worked," he continued, "as a clapboard boy on *To Be or Not to Be*, the delightful Ernst Lubitsch's wartime comedy that Jack did with Carole Lombard. He was marvelous. They both were, of course. Even doing the show within the show performance of *Hamlet*. He could have been anyone. Did anything. Had, well, at least the career of an actor like Walter Matthau."

"Fred Jackson, Academy Award–winning cinematographer," Jackie continued, "worked as a camera assistant on Jack Benny's last film, *The Horn Blows at Midnight*."

"Jack was a real professional," Fred boomed, causing those around him to wince. "I remember I was changing some film cartridges. You had to keep your hands in this dark bag, you see, when you were pulling the exposed film out of the magazines. Jack would come over and kid me, you know, the way people do. He'd accuse me of stealing money from him, you know. Of course he played this terrible tightwad. And he'd say things. Well, I can't remember what they were exactly. But oh, they'd make you scream. Hell . . ."

"Make that *heck* the next time, Fred," Celestine ordered.

"I thought *The Horn Blows at Midnight* was a very funny little film," Fred went on heedlessly. "Nothing wrong with it. Good laughs. I mean, Jack Benny in a sheet with a halo and angel wings. That's pretty funny, right?"

"George Burns," Jackie continued, "Jack Benny's good friend, thought the comedian shortchanged himself when he always kidded about his movie career."

"Y'know," Marcus launched into his George Burns voice. It wasn't as spot-on as the others, but it was plenty good enough. "Jack was actually pretty good. He just couldn't resist a funny gag. Even when it was on himself. Sweet guy, Jack Benny. My best friend for fifty years. We never had a quarrel. I loved the guy. Every time he saw me he laughed. How can you beat that? If you're a comedian. Anyway, I was always playing gags on him. One time I got Jerry Lewis to go in on a practical joke with me. Jerry told Jack that I was in London, complaining about being lonely. So Jack should send me, y'see, an expensive tie, beautifully gift-wrapped, with a scented perfumed note saying, 'From an anonymous admirer.' Said it would drive me crazy. Little did he know, right? So this goes on for a few weeks. I'm playing the Palladium. Every week I'm getting a beautiful new tie and Jack's back home, convinced he's driving me loco. Finally I telegraph him, 'Jack. Thanks for the ties. I got enough now. How about switching to silk socks?' "

While Marcus put his invisible cigar back in his mouth, Jackie continued, "Another good friend, despite their ersatz long-running feud, was the comedian Fred Allen."

"Hollywood," nasally rasped Ralph Stevens, another dog-show contact of Jackie's—a round little man who just naturally sounded like Fred Allen—"is a great place if you're an orange. You know, I am working on a new cellophane sheet of music. This will enable song warblers to look through their music and see how people are reacting to their efforts. Many times an entertainer is singing his heart out and behind his music, guests are holding their noses or doing acrostics. With the cellophane music sheet the guest will know that the soloist can see him and he will act accordingly. I have another invention for unfunny comedians. Jack Benny, take note. This is a timed stink bomb that explodes in the lobby as the guests walk out on the comedian, and the odor drives the guests back into the theater until the comedian finishes his act."

"Fred Allen's show," Jackie continued, "was on at eight-thirty, a half hour after Jack's. At first Fred's program was more popular than Benny's."

"We have an advertising executive from the Sal-Hepatica people over to visit us today," Stevens/Allen continued on cue. "I'll tell you, this fellow is good at his job and happy to have it. Loves board meetings with his fellow advertising execs, or so they tell me. When our friend went to Colgate, you see, he was an All-American quarterback. And when a quarterback stands behind the line with the linemen stooped over, well, he's got about the same view as he's got right now."

"But," Jackie continued, "too many jokes against his sponsors . . ."

"Hair-Return, the magic new solution from those Merlins of modern magic at Winston Industries," Stevens/Allen pounced on his cue, "promises that regular doses of its product on a gentleman's bald pate will restore a luxuriant crop of healthy brown hair. Well, that sounds unlikely, doesn't it? And if you gents want to slop gallons of the stuff on your gleaming little domes, far be it from me to discourage you. But why not embrace your unmanly affliction? Look at the bright side. Take a look at a baby. Nothing is younger than a baby. And nothing has less hair. As a matter of fact I think it is the baby's baldness that gives it that youthful appearance. So, throw away your crutches, bald eagles. Stay bald. Shave it all off and look forty years younger today."

"And too many jokes," Jackie continued, "about sensitive political issues."

"Mussolini . . . Italian fellow," Stevens/Allen snarled. "You may have heard of him. It seems they found him dead recently. Strung up by his admirers. What a break for the devil, eh? At last he has a straight man."

"And," Jackie continued, "too many jokes at the expense of the 'nabobs,' as he liked to call them, who ran the networks and radio itself."

"With few exceptions," Ralph/Fred orated, "radio is a bog of mediocrity where little men with carbon-copy minds wallow around in a sluice of their own making."

"And . . ." Jackie flipped the page.

"Several of the network great poobahs and high nabobs came out to see me this week," Stevens/Allen related. "They decided to leave their wives, mistresses, and comfortable New York corporate headquarters to assist me in my efforts to offer a corking good show every week on a budget of ten dollars and sixteen cents. Their help consisted of counting my paper clips and stomping on my best jokes with both feet. I urged them to return to their tree-bestrewn big city headquarters. How could the woods of Gotham survive with all the saps in Hollywood?"

"Finally," Jackie continued, "Fred Allen put his standing on the network in a precarious position. At the urging of his friend Jack Benny, America's favorite intellectual comedian launched a feud."

"Before shoes were invented," Stevens/Allen attacked, "Jack Benny was a heel. I don't want to say that the

Waukegan Methuselah is cheap, but he's got short arms and carries his money low in his pockets."

Jackie and Celestine exchanged winks. "Jack Benny fought back."

"Listening to Fred Allen," Dunn/Benny responded, "is like listening to two Abbotts and no Costello."

"When Jack Benny plays the violin, it sounds as if the strings are still in the cat."

"Fred Allen is so tight, when he finally spent a five-dollar bill, Lincoln's eyes were bloodshot."

"Benny's got no more hair than an elbow."

"Allen looks like a short butcher peeking over two pounds of liver."

Jackie continued, "They started appearing together at benefits."

"Welcome to the March of Dimes Benefit, Fred."

"Hah, the dime hasn't been minted that could march past you, Jack."

"And . . ."

"Welcome to the Los Angeles Music Center, Jack."

"Thank you, Fred. It's wonderful to do benefit shows like this with so many celebrities. I'm sitting up here on the dais, you know, so I don't have to buy a ticket—they're so expensive—and I look around me and see all these big stars. Bob Hope, Bing Crosby. I thought I saw Jane Russell, so of course I put on my glasses. You can imagine how disappointed I was when I saw it was Fred Allen here. You see the bags under his eyes are so low . . ."

"Most wonderful of all," Jackie continued, "were their guest shots on each other's shows."

"And my special guest tonight is Fred Allen."

"Was that my cue, Benny? I couldn't hear you over the clicking of your false teeth. You know, Benny went to see the Colosseum in Rome last month. 'Not bad,' was his comment, 'if you like modern.'"

"And . . ."

"Tonight these groaning boards are fixing to bear the weight of America's Silas Marner. I refer of course to Jack 'Buck' Benny."

"Thank you, Fred. I heard you just completed your last movie. Is it true that you have such high blood pressure that in Technicolor you photograph plaid?"

"Not bad, Benny. But we'll avoid a war of wits. You couldn't ad-lib a belch after a Hungarian dinner."

"You wouldn't say that," Dunn/Benny replied, "if my writers were here."

The rehearsal concluded satisfactorily and Jackie reluctantly rose at once to go.

"Leaving us so soon?" Ronald Dunn inquired in his deep, sexy voice.

"I'm afraid I have to," Jackie replied, genuinely reluctant to go.

"Investigating another murder?"

"Unfortunately."

"Can we get together some time and compare alibis?"

"Call me," Jackie replied, blushing. She started to rush out and leave everyone thinking that they knew something she wasn't sure she knew herself. Jackie then abruptly turned around and came back. "Ron, I'm going to a party. Would you like to come along as my escort?"

"Love to!" Dunn said at once. He then took the pressure off the moment by cracking, "As Benny would say, 'Free Food. Free Drink. What's not to like?' "

"I'll even drive," Jackie offered.

"Wonderful," Dunn announced, slipping easily into a familiar Benny posture. "You know how I like to buy gas one gallon at a time."

Jackie was waiting in the foyer of Celestine's large home, consciously modeled after the Selznick conception of Manderly. Ronald Dunn, looking very handsome in a light Burberry raincoat and tan gabardines, joined her after a moment.

"Sorry to keep you."

Jackie looked at Dunn gratefully. There weren't many men who could have deflected such a potentially embarrassing exit so gracefully. "I'm glad you're coming, Ron."

Dunn gave her one of his wicked leers and replied, "I am too." As he followed her out to her car, Dunn pattered, "You know, I do have my Lamborghini here. I could drive. You could lie back on the soft velvet cushions with your eyes closed, feeling the gentle strength and power of a big . . ."

Jackie laughed as she unlocked her passenger side door. "Watch the dog hair getting in."

They sped through the twisting streets between Celestine's big house and Dean Foreman's home until they were stopped by a small but impenetrable knot of cars that had slowed to watch a fat man take out his garbage.

"Well, I know I'm in the Midwest now." Dunn lifted his voice so it carried strongly through the open passenger window. "Look at those drivers ahead of us, grazing like field stock."

The car owners, apparently hearing the voice of the one-time TV master spy, sheepishly sped up.

Jackie looked lovingly at Dunn's classic profile. He even cursed half-witted drivers the way she did. What a man.

"Is that what they're slowing down for?" Dunn asked incredulously after craning his neck. "They were so entranced by a guy with a bad body putting his empty beer cans and potato chip bags on the curb? My goodness, this country is starved for entertainment."

Jackie smiled and they rode in silence for a moment.

"So," Dunn fished for compliments. "How was the reading?"

"Terrific," Jackie replied gladly. "You were remarkable. How long have you been doing Benny?"

"All my life," Dunn replied, happy for the straight line. "It's just recently I've been smart enough to get paid for it."

"How's the one-man show going?"

"Good," Dunn responded, so enthusiastic that Jackie knew he meant okay.

"How are the crowds?"

"Mostly sellouts," Dunn replied quickly, "but then I'm not getting those Riverfront Stadium gigs. Old Jack is too esoteric for that, I guess."

"That's a shame," Jackie replied genuinely.

"Well," Dunn sighed, "it's not like I wasn't warned. The booking service that sends you out on these things cautions you—only Holbrook and Whitmore get the concert halls and opera houses. And they don't go out so much anymore. Probably not entirely by their own choice. I hope before this is over to do Lincoln Center for two weeks, maybe the Folger in Washington and if I'm very lucky, the Ahmanson back home. Here in Palmer, I'm appearing on the dark Mondays at the Playhouse on the Park."

"Don't take it personally," Jackie urged.

"Oh, I don't," Dunn replied, holding on to the hang strap as Jackie took a corner sharply. "I know that no matter how often the newspapers claim that there's a vast audience out there for culture, that when it actually comes to getting Ward and June out of those robes and Stratoloungers, it's not that easy."

"And the money. We are in a depression, after all."

"Well," Dunn shrugged. "This isn't New York or LA. We're only talking twenty dollars."

"That's three movie tickets around here, bub," Jackie informed the actor. "And according to the papers, the average Palmer parent over thirty averages exactly three movies a year."

Dunn nodded. "So if they come to see me pretend to play a violin, they've blown their annual wad."

"That's about the size of it," Jackie agreed, looking to maneuver through another morass.

"Well, you have my sympathy, people," Dunn yelled out the window. "It must be a terrible burden to own a Department of Motor Vehicles license and not actually know how to drive."

Jackie maneuvered the Jeep past a vehicle with an elderly driver wearing a hat and holding an oversize steering wheel. In so doing, she narrowly missed a gawking man who had been taking out his garbage when he stopped to regard what the cars were doing out on the street in front of his house.

"So, did you do much radio yourself, Ron?" Jackie asked.

"No," Dunn replied, running a hand back over the widow's peak of his hair. "Mostly local Philadelphia stuff as a kid. What did I do that you might have heard of? Let's see. I was on *Lux Radio Presents*, but after Cecil B. De Mille left the show."

"Who was doing it? Martin Gabel?"

"Very good," Dunn replied, genuinely impressed. "To be brutally honest with you, I got that part because Gabel and I had the same dentist on Broad Street. We were both in the waiting room. Doc Herman hadn't put out any magazines, so I was proofreading my résumé, mostly lies at that point. You know the sorts of things actors try to get away with. 'Yes, I played Macbeth. Crowds seemed to like it.' Whenever I said, 'Is that a dagger I see before me?' half the audience used to always yell, 'Yes!' "

"Ho, ho," Jackie responded.

"And then they'd say, 'That's fine. But where did you say you played this part, Mr. Dunn?' 'Oh, a little theater,' I'd say. 'You've never heard of it. Out in Lancaster, PA. Amish country. Had the old candlestick footlights. It was so dark I kept tripping over my broadsword. Might as well have been playing Othello.' "

Jackie laughed again, but commented, "Why do I feel I'm not the first one to hear these stories?"

"Hey," Dunn protested with mock innocence. "Just to make it good for you, I polished these jokes on Carson. And you know he was a much tougher audience than Leno."

"Anyway . . . ?"

"Martin Gabel, having nothing better to do, read over my shoulder. He saw I had a list of apocryphal credits as long as your arm and said"—Dunn stuck his finger in his mouth and talked as if in the grips of a horrible toothache—" 'Thay, do you wanth to thplay a kid on my radio pwogwam?' I said, 'Thwure,' and a radio career was born."

"Sort of brings a tear to the eye," commented Jackie wryly.

"Oh, my radio career made for plenty of crying. I did one of the last *I Love a Mystery* shows. A succulent non-Thanksgiving turkey about some guy who kills a fellow with microwaves. I played a kid who accidentally caught the murderer using his secret device on film with my little Kodak. So the murderer sent his trusty retriever to break into my house and steal the camera film and all before the detectives got there."

Jackie responded distractedly as she maneuvered around a station wagon with a ladder tied on to each side. "What did Doc and Jack make of that?"

Dunn laughed. "I don't think they were still with the show at the time. I think the boys' milkman was solving the crimes by that time. Or maybe their mothers."

At that point the Jeep pulled up in front of Algernon Foreman's house.

"That was such a terrific ride," Dunn announced, "I have to kiss you."

"If you must, you must," Jackie acquiesced.

"You know," Dunn whispered in Jackie's ear, "I have a hotel bed so big you could place a person at each corner of the diagonal and they could comfortably stretch their arms and grasp each other around the wrists the way the sky divers did in *The Gypsy Moths*. Now that's not exactly my idea of a good time but if you were to come back with me . . ."

Jackie laughed explosively and pushed Dunn away. "Watch the dog hair getting out."

Accepting Dunn's cynical offer of an arm to appear on, Jackie and Ronald walked in through the open front door of the Foreman home.

"Hi. Glad you could make it," a woman with a tray of drinks greeted them. It was clear by her tone that she didn't recognize either Jackie or the handsome fiftyish former television star. Jackie couldn't get too worked up, since she only vaguely recognized the server herself. She didn't remember the prematurely gray-haired young woman's name, but knew she taught Chaucer.

"Do you desire drink?" the woman asked absentmindedly. "It's cool say I and packs a fearful wallop."

"What is it?" Jackie asked.

"Fresca and white wine," the woman replied.

"That sounds great," Jackie said delightedly.

"Make it two," Dunn piped up, running his hand lightly up the back of Jackie's silk blouse.

"Now you be good," Jackie demanded insincerely. "Come inside."

"Love to."

"I'll introduce you," Jackie said quickly, "to the local intelligentsia."

"I hope you'll translate."

Jackie gave Dunn a suspicious look. "Just a minute, you. Didn't I read somewhere that you have a law degree?"

"You've been boning up on me," Dunn said archly. "How wonderful. Actually, dear Jacqueline, the truth of the matter was, the early fifties was a terrific time to bribe your way past the boards. Only set Pater back a couple of thousand."

"None of that," Jackie said firmly, putting her hand on Dunn's chest and suppressing the thrills. "You are handsome, witty, wonderful, and I am absolutely on my guard. You will get no sympathy from me at all tonight."

"It's not sympathy I want from you, Jackie," Dunn replied quietly, plucking at a lock of Jackie's hair, then slowly letting it fall.

"Follow me."

"To the ends of the earth."

As the couple left, the Chaucer lady said to a friend, "I *like* him."

The Foreman study was male territory. Graham Grosset, the great Catholic novelist, whose work ranged from Great Anglican literature like *The Tale of the Gorgonzola* to exciting espionage thrillers like *Government Under a Cloud*, held the floor, as he usually did in parties of this kind. Grosset had come to Palmer as a guest lecturer and, at former Communications Chairman Philip Barger's insistence, to oversee the making of his great Kestrel trilogy into a motion picture. Barger had died and with him had gone the plan to make the movie.

Grosset had cheerfully weathered the loss of his patron, the loss of his movie adaptation, and, worst of all, a terrific scandal when it was revealed that two of the three books of the trilogy had been plagiarized from the great Portuguese epic poet Paolo Gilberto. Faced with utter ruin and humiliation, Graham Grosset had not only survived, he had triumphed. The fact that he had been pilloried by the critics endeared him to his students, and encouraged by a NEA grant, Grosset wrote his autobiography, *Creature of Fraud,* which the American public responded to characteristically. Informed on every page that they had been lied to and cheated, they revenged themselves by standing on long lines to buy the book and then lustily sing its praises.

Grosset, who loved to come to Dean Foreman's literary fests and hold court, was expounding on his favorite subject. "To me, it's fascinating," he was saying. "The whole idea of forgery or counterfeiting. Of hoaxes, even. Of doing something that is not genuine and having it taken for something other than what it truly is. Isn't that after all what fiction's all about?"

Jackie sat down on the arm of an unoccupied lounge chair. As much as she wanted to talk to Henry Obermaier, Jackie, the eternal student, was fascinated with some of the points that Graham Grosset could make when he was really on.

"In the art world," Grosset began, "nothing is more vexing than the question of reality. We want to know, don't we, that the painting we're spending thirteen million dollars for is really a Picasso or Matisse or whoever it is that you're rich enough to buy. Which raises the whole question of 'Realism' in the art world. What does that mean, 'Realism'? That's a whole movement, you know. I find that absurd, really. 'Realism,' you see, is a painting that looks real. That appears to be real. And of course the fact is, it's not real. That it's an obvious illusion—a splendidly executed painting—is the reason it's so valuable."

As an enthralled Jackie absorbed this information, Ronald Dunn crept up to her. "Is this one of those sit-around-and-listen parties? Should I get us a plate of hors d'oeuvres to nibble on?"

"Sure," Jackie responded, absently patting the great screen lover.

"There would be no point," Grosset continued, after a pause for a sherry throat-wetting, "to forging a Da Vinci unless there was a market for such a work. Painters before Leonardo often painted on large immovable

surfaces. Leonardo hit on the idea of making art port-
able—thus creating in one fell swoop both the art and
the forger's industry. What was the point of forgery in
the art world before that? You could paint your local
cathedral's ceiling as beautifully as Michelangelo painted the Sistine's, but to what purpose? Everyone knew
Michelangelo only painted one ceiling. But a single
piece of art, framed not so it could be put on a wall,
but so it could be more conveniently carried on an ass,
who knew if it was genuine or real?

"Leonardo didn't always sign his paintings and when
he did, he did so in a bold distinctive hand. Easiest thing
in the world for a forger to imitate. Far less difficult
to imitate than his beautiful faces. As my good friend
Wyndham Lewis once said, 'When you forge a signature, you don't do it by modifying your handwriting into
resembling another's, but by abandoning handwriting
altogether. You turn the model upside down and draw
what you see.' "

Dunn returned at that moment, and Jackie was glad to
see that he sat down at once and started listening without demanding attention for himself. This Ronald Dunn,
Jackie thought to herself, was a rare man indeed.

"This whole question about what is worthwhile,"
Grosset continued. "What is valuable in art is a very
vexing question indeed. Picasso's signature, for instance,
may make a painting more valuable than another work
and yet, I recall standing next to Pablo in a Spanish
police station one day. A man had been arrested for
forging Picasso's name and passing off his own work
as that of the great master. Picasso examined the work
at length and then said finally, 'I wish I'd done that.'

"What's this obsession we have with proving that
a pleasing piece of work is authentic? What does it
matter? A forger, after all, does good work. He sells it
however as the work of another. When it is discovered,
as it invariably is, the value of the work plummets.

Often the painting is branded worthless and yet it is still good work.

"A clever forger does not copy a painting that is known to exist. He paints in the style of the artist he is copying, a work that did not before exist. You may say—and people have said—'Gee, I don't generally like Renoir but that one I like.' And you are buying a forgery. What are the value systems there?

"Art is not always widely appreciated. The most beloved works of art in the history of the world are appreciated by about twelve percent of the population. That may amount to hundreds of millions over the years, but never more than about twelve percent of the people on earth at any one time. Classicists tear their hair. How could you not appreciate Shakespeare, Shaw, Wilson, Beethoven, or Bach? Well, part of that is each generation needs to have the great works of the past translated anew for its own time.

"In the great bardic tradition you know, writers were not endlessly pressured to come up with something new. No, just the opposite. In fact, having to do something new was considered a tremendous cop-out. A tremendous lack of face. Like starting your own baseball league instead of working through the ranks of the minor leagues to take your cuts against the majors.

"You showed what you were made of—your stuff, so to speak—by taking a shot at the classics. An Arthurian tale, Troilus and Cressida, Tristan and Isolde, Pyramus and Thisbe, a Ulysses who becomes Jason, then Sinbad, then Captain Blood, and then so brilliantly in the hands of James Joyce, he becomes Ulysses again, no longer an intrepid warrior straddling the globe, but an overweight pub goer snoring in his bed, dreaming of adultery and watered liquor. Ms. Walsh, welcome!"

Grosset held his glass of sherry high, clearly as much interested in resting his throat for a moment as in being polite to Jackie.

"Professor. You're on a roll tonight."

"Well, coming from a woman whose specialty is apparently *ham* rolls, that's a very dubious compliment, I must say."

Jackie joined in the general laughter. "Actually, those are my mother's contributions to the festivities. We had some left from our last poker game."

"Most tasty," Grosset averred loudly. "As is your radio script, by all accounts. Here is a splendid example of what I'm talking about. Ms. Walsh has done a radio script. The fact that such a medium is no longer popular does not make it any less artistic." Grosset then turned to a small knot of listeners, singling out one for his attention.

"Henry, do you know our Ms. Walsh? Teacher, mother, amateur detective, bearer of leftover hors d'oeuvres. If it is true that we are going through another dark age, it is Renaissance women like Jacqueline Walsh who we must count on to lead us toward the light."

Henry Obermaier, who had been biding his time before taking Graham Grosset aside, turned to regard Jackie. They had met twice, once shortly after Jackie had been rehired as an instructor in Communications and once many years before at her father's funeral. During most of his last few years in office, President Obermaier had been an odious, slightly muddleheaded administrator whom trustees like Stuart Goodwillie had used as a doormat. When the tainted water that the Rodgers president had consumed by the gallon had finally been cleared up, it gave the world a chance to see a whole new Henry Obermaier—and led to his imminent departure from Rodgers.

"Of course I remember Ms. Walsh," rumbled the big man. "How are you, Jackie?"

Put at ease by the familiarity of the famed administrator, Jackie replied comfortably, "I'm fine, Henry. How are you?"

"Wonderful. Just wonderful. You look well." Obermaier's eyes traveled briefly to Ronald Dunn, wondering if the two were together and if an introduction was in order.

Dunn took the pressure off Jackie by striking up a conversation with Millie Brooks, Jackie's friend who taught Sex in Literature and Children's Literature for the university.

"Thank you," Jackie responded, rising to her feet and walking over to the former president. "You've lost some weight."

"Yes." When Henry Obermaier saw Grosset disappear into a crowd of admirers, he turned and gave Jackie his full attention.

Jackie then noticed that Obermaier's new closely trimmed Vandyke went very well with his now thinner, lined face.

"So what brings you to this den of iniquity?" Obermaier asked. "I won't try to disguise my motives. I'm trying to drag off at least a few of Rodgers' top people to come east with me."

"Actually, I'm here mostly to talk to you."

"Really? Don't tell me you're looking for a job? I'd love to have you."

Dunn gave a look over.

"No. I think my place is here in Palmer. At least for right now." Jackie sneaked a look back at Dunn. His head was averted. She turned back to Obermaier. "Actually, Henry, I'm interested in talking to you about what happened on the night Mannheim Goodwillie was killed."

"Oh." Clearly Obermaier didn't find the topic all that interesting. "That will take five minutes."

"Well, perhaps I'll have a few questions. Can we go somewhere?"

"Sure," Obermaier agreed readily. "Give me a chance to grab a cigarette."

They reluctantly left the room just as Grosset was standing up again. "You see, we chaps in England don't much like to let on that we have an imagination. You've heard of Romantic Literature, how each book started with a little author's introduction purporting that the tale you were about to read was an actual happenstance— that the author was an eyewitness or had found journals or letters to back up the truth of what he wrote? Dean Swift's *Tale of the Tub* was thought to be an actual happening. The book never carried his name on it and he denied its authorship his whole life. People didn't write novels—they wrote fictional diaries. Readers of the time thought that what they were reading was real. A very dangerous thing to believe, by the way, for when you can't distinguish fiction from fact, it's often difficult to distinguish right from wrong. Believe me, I know whereof I speak . . ."

Jackie and Obermaier tore themselves away with difficulty.

Noting that the living-room scene was almost identical to the study—except that it was Paolo Cook holding court—Jackie led Obermaier to the back of the large front hall. There was a quiet space near the stairs where the coat closet was located. The area was big enough for a padded wooden bench, rescued from the old Rodgers library, and a suit of armor, allegedly the very suit of stage armor John Barrymore had worn when he played Richard III. Jackie sat on the bench. Obermaier took a wooden match from the cup clenched in Richard III's left hand and lit a cigarette.

"So?" he said.

"I suppose the police have asked you what you saw?" Jackie began.

"I spoke to a Lieutenant McGowan," Obermaier replied. "He was most respectful."

Jackie smiled privately. She knew that McGowan didn't like Henry Obermaier at all. "And I suppose you've read what the Palmer *Gazette* said about you and Mannheim Goodwillie?"

Obermaier nodded. "Yeah. I was born in this town, Jackie. I've lived here and worked here all my life. I won't pretend that my tenure as president of Rodgers University was the greatest thing that ever happened to this fair community, but it seems that I did more good than harm and I'm more than a little disappointed that this is going to be my send-off, a kick in the butt out of town under a cloud of scandal over things that happened forty years ago. Do you want to hear about it?"

Jackie nodded.

"I joined the army in 1954," Obermaier started, puffing furiously on his cigarette to keep it lit. "The Korean conflict was still going then, although it was winding down. I didn't fit in very well with my fellow enlisted men. I was a college boy. I read history books in my spare time instead of drinking bootleg hooch or playing stud poker. I got into a couple of fights in basic training camp and they threw me out of the service with a section eight discharge. It can mean anything at all. In my case, it just meant that I didn't fit in.

"I came back here to Palmer, eventually became a history teacher, and served, as people did in those days, as a volunteer on the college admissions committee. Although it was a lot of work, it eventually led to me getting into admissions full-time, then other administration posts and finally the presidency. For a long time it was unrewarding work. Especially when you had to thumbs-down some student who wanted to get into one of the special programs. That's how I ran afoul of Mannheim Goodwillie."

Obermaier paused to touch a high-stream lighter to a cigarette, then resumed. "Twenty years ago, believe it or not, Mannheim was considered the tyrant of the Goodwillie family and Stuart was known as 'Mr. Softy.' Well, Mannheim had separated from his wife at this time and was courting a widow with a college-age son. He wanted this boy to get into a special chemistry program we had. It was a small program, partly financed by the Defense Department. Early polymer work, as it happens, which much later, in other places, became the basis of today's cartridge disk technology."

"Really? I hadn't heard that."

"Yes," Obermaier responded icily. "You'll notice the good work we do here at Rodgers doesn't get quite the same play as our little scandals. Anyway, the special classes were taught by an old German named Bayer. He liked small classes and the labs were just tiny. The equipment was so expensive you could only get a couple of each of the separating machines and some of these were prototypes which kept breaking down. So to make a long story short, hundreds of students applied for these programs every year and only two or three were accepted.

"Mannheim's potential stepson simply didn't qualify. And the frustrating thing was, much as Mannheim Goodwillie wanted this boy to get into these classes and bring whatever knowledge he would gain with him when he came to work for Falk & Goodwillie after graduation, the boy didn't actually have any interest in the subject. You could tell just by talking to him. But you couldn't buck Falk & Goodwillie in those days. Even though the admissions committee unanimously agreed that the boy was not a viable candidate, nobody wanted to tell Mannheim Goodwillie that he wasn't going to get what he wanted. Finally, I told him and the man made the next two years of my life a living hell.

"He hired private detectives and they distorted my military record to the point where you would have thought I was the Manchurian Candidate. They found out that I had taken advantage of some free university psychological therapy—I was trying to lose weight and quit smoking even then . . ." Obermaier paused to light another cigarette. "And Goodwillie tried to get me thrown out. Even after he and the woman whose son had started the whole mess broke up, he still hounded me. Fortunately for me, he and Stuart had a falling out over another woman . . ."

"Jane Bellamy."

"Yes." Obermaier gave Jackie a sharp look, as if wondering who had told her, then resumed. "Anyway, so Stuart backed me just to torment his brother and I managed to survive by the skin of my teeth."

"Is Arthur Goodwillie, the one who died recently . . . ?"

Obermaier nodded. "Mannheim's son. The old man and his wife were eventually reconciled. Mostly for Arthur's sake, I suppose. I was sorry to hear about Arthur's accident. He was a student of mine. Good kid."

"Potential historian?" Jackie asked.

Obermaier laughed. "Actually, I had Arthur in Driver's Ed. My first year teaching. He was a senior. Wonderful driver. Was surprised to hear he died in an automobile accident. That's the last way I would have expected that young man to go. But that's all tainted water under the bridge. I should go home and pack. I've got half-full boxes everywhere."

Jackie nodded. "Thanks for your help, Henry. And there's nothing you can tell me that might help the police catch this murderer?"

Obermaier shook his head and dropped his cigarette butt in through the visor of the helmet of the Richard III. "No, can't think of a thing. I was as surprised as anybody. Thought it was natural causes. Goodwillie was no spring chicken."

"I know."

"Whoever it was, I hope you catch him." Obermaier opened the cloak closet and withdrew his coat and hat. "Whatever happened between Mannheim and me was over a long time ago. I won't say there weren't any hard feelings, but you saw him. Those years in Florida had really mellowed the man. He was almost likable. And whatever he tried to do to me, he didn't succeed. I've had a very successful life, all things considered. If you come right down to it, I've probably had a better life than he did."

Obermaier left the party and Jackie drifted back into the main room. She heard Paolo Cook's voice.

"Graham Grosset, of course, is a part of the great literary tradition going back to the sixteenth century. Going back to *Don Quixote*, in fact. You know, the first volume of *Quixote* was so popular that the public clamored for more. Gutenberg had just invented the printing press and all these noble stories of love and knightly valor were coming out. They had inspired Cervantes to write his *Quixote* and now pressured his publisher to get into the next installment.

"Sixteenth-century writers, like them or not, were nothing if not prolific. The most prolific playwrights and novelists in history were working out of Spain and Portugal during this period. Anyway, in 1614, just a year before the second volume of Cervantes's *Don Quixote* was published, there appeared what is called 'the apocryphal Quixote' or 'the false Quixote.' It was in fact a volume claiming to complete the adventures begun by Cervantes. These adventures were completed by somebody else. The real author, whoever he may be, put a pseudonym on the piece, Alonzo Fernandez de Avilinea. No one knows who he was.

"Different scholars have different theories. I favor the one giving credit to my old friend the Portuguese epic poet Paolo Gilberto. Others favor Cervantes himself. In any case, this spurious volume not only claimed to be an authorized continuation of the first book, in addition, the author went on to make scurrilous remarks about Cervantes. A fairly ungracious way to react unless the author was Cervantes himself having a little fun at his own expense.

"Perhaps it was an author Cervantes's publisher financed, as another theory goes, to pressure his star author to continue the series. If that was the intent it succeeded admirably and the second volume of *Quixote* opens with the knight and his squire reacting to the publication of the first volume. And if that's not a 1990s literary situation, I don't know what is. Quixote hears that he has been written about. He hears in fact that his adventures are something of a best-seller. Eventually Quixote and Sancho learn that there is also this fraudulent account, that there is this version of their story that is not accurate, that is not true, that is a gross and horrible fiction. So that most of their subsequent tribulations and misadventures came about directly because they are trying to prove to an uncaring world that they are not what they are portrayed to be. That they are not fictional characters on unbelievable quests, but real.

"Fairly sophisticated concept for a book written almost four hundred years ago in the very first days of the novel, isn't it?"

"That's interesting," Bill Reigert, the young magician who had earlier been at Jackie's reading, commented. He was one of Paolo Cook's most interested listeners. "The point you make about reality and illusion, I mean. It's a major part of the act I have with my sister."

"Of course," Paolo nodded in approval. "And so it should be. Reality and illusion is the theme of the *Quixote*. It is in so many ways what the book is about. And one of the, shall we say, ongoing charms of the book is to see how often our hero will batter his head against reality. How strongly he is convinced of the quality of the value of his dream."

"Excuse me, Bill," Jackie reluctantly interrupted. "I have to go now. Do you still need that ride?"

The handsome magician at once jumped to his feet. "Yes, Jackie. Thank you." Bill pumped Paolo's hand. "Paolo, a most interesting evening. Thank you. Thank you very much."

"Glad you could make it."

"I'm glad Jackie invited me," Bill smiled. "Actually I invited myself when I heard there was someone here who was going to talk *Don Quixote* and she agreed. A fascinating book for a magician, believe me. Slowly but surely my sister and I keep building up the Knight of the Mirrors part of our show. It threatens one day to overwhelm the card tricks and actually become the entire performance."

"Well, it sounds fascinating," Paolo responded politely. "I'm sure Sara and Isaac will be delighted to hear we have passes and I look forward to seeing your show."

As Paolo moved off, Bill turned back to Jackie. "Another moment?" he asked. "I just want to call Lil. Tell her I'm coming."

Jackie smiled. "If she's your twin, doesn't she know?"

Bill happily returned the smile. "We hate to squander our psychic energies on miscellanea. Be right back."

"Meet you in the front hall," Jackie called after him. Jackie gathered the red sweater her mother had knitted for her tighter around her shoulders. Dean Foreman didn't have the heat on and the evening had turned cold and rainy. Attracted by the warmth of the noted author's voice, Jackie listened while she waited.

A dead soldier sherry bottle lay on one side on the floor by his foot, but the glib Grosset was still going strong. "What does a writer write, after all, but a sort of prose music? If you have a voice, and an ear, you can make a book on most any topic interesting. Look at my Nobel Prize-winning Kestrel trilogy, for instance. Purloined plot or no, those books positively sing. If anyone in the room is looking for modesty, he should look elsewhere, obviously. I am in love with my own writing, and why not? You can survive without a musical ear but at what price? Most find it odd that Franz Kafka had absolutely no ear for music. I wouldn't have thought otherwise. I find it positively astounding though that W. B. Yeats was tone deaf. Amazing that a poet could survive let alone thrive with such a handicap."

Jackie finally succeeded in making eye contact with Ronald Dunn. She wiggled her fingers at him.

Dunn put his fingers to his jaws in a Jack Benny attitude of extreme surprise and dismay.

Jackie pointed to her watch and then put her hands to her head as if to mime sleeping on a pillow.

Dunn then touched his own chest and pointed to her and then made a motion as if sawing a violin.

Jackie laughed and made a big no-way gesture with her arms and then at that moment Bill Reigert came back.

"Hi. Sorry to keep you."

"Quite all right," Jackie responded, embarrassed, jumping around to face him.

"Something wrong?"

"I'm so tired I'm yawning weird," Jackie replied.

"Oh," Bill replied dubiously. "Okay."

They walked outside and down to the wet street where Jackie's Jeep was parked.

"What happened to our beautiful weather?" Bill asked as the rain started to plaster his long sandy brown hair.

"Presto chango," replied Jackie. "I heard some clown on TV blaming a Philippine volcano."

"I hope," Bill responded in a whimsical English accent, "this isn't simply a matter of the bloody wogs forgetting to sacrifice the odd virgin. One does so hate it when one's juju man lays down on the job."

"Bill, really."

"Sorry." Bill smiled as they struggled into their seat-belt harnesses. "I've had a few and am feeling a little bit goofy."

"Just don't palm my keys, or something."

"Would I do that?" Bill smiled.

"I've never known a magician who could resist that one," Jackie replied. She then looked into her purse, saw that her keys were missing, looked up, and saw them residing in Bill Reigert's hand.

"How many magicians have you known?" Bill dropped his voice sexily.

"All I care to," Jackie snapped, grabbing the keys. Actually, Jackie had never dated a single magician and found the idea oddly exciting. But although she found Bill Reigert more than a little bit handsome, she had enough on her hands with Michael McGowan and Ronald Dunn now.

It was dark and rainy and Jackie was so tired and distracted that she almost crashed into the big car blocking Ward Clement Drive.

A little shook up, Jackie was immediately out the door and raging at the driver, "Are you crazy!? Are you driving away from the lunatic asylum with your arms in a straitjacket?" Jackie then saw that the driver of the limousine was Stuart Goodwillie's man Carnero. He was wet, despite his dark, wide-brimmed gaucho's hat, and he had a gun.

"Please. Get into the van. Mr. Goodwillie wants to talk to you. Now."

Jackie threw her head back indignantly. "And what am I supposed to do with my Jeep? Just leave it here in the middle of the road? So people can run into it? The way I almost did with you just now?"

Carnero pointed with his pistol to Jackie's passenger. "Your friend can drive it home."

Bill Reigert got out of the car and leaned back with his arms crossed negligently against the hood. "Sorry old chap," Bill again affected a fop English accent, "I can't drive, you see?"

Carnero gave Reigert a look that said he did not entirely trust him, then shifted his gaze to Jackie. "Park your truck at the curb there. I'll drive you back later."

"It is not a truck and I am doing no such thing," Jackie responded firmly. "I am not about to leave my car on the street in some strange neighborhood and go off to some mansion to be grilled all night by some vindictive old prune of a millionaire. I'm tired and I have a full schedule tomorrow. If your boss wants to make an appointment, he can leave a message for me at the university. I'll call him when I can and tell him when it will be convenient for me to meet with him."

"I think you don't hear so good, *sí*?" Carnero flicked at Jackie's temple lock with the barrel of his pistol. "You come with me now, as I say."

"Now, I say, dear chap," Reigert raised his voice. "I think you should put away that gun right now and leave this woman strictly alone or . . ."

Carnero turned the barrel of the pistol toward Bill Reigert. "Or?"

Reigert held out his hand and a half deck of cards came flying out.

Carnero, startled, stumbled backward.

Quickly materializing two throwing cards, Reigert flipped them with deadly precision, knocking the pistol out of Carnero's hand.

Jackie came up with the fallen gun and pointed it at Carnero. "Don't move."

Carnero easily reached out and pulled it from Jackie's fingers before the inexperienced markswoman could disengage the safeties. Jackie silently cursed the stifling laws that made it so difficult in this dangerous age to own and become proficient with a protective handgun.

"Now!" Carnero was starting to become angry, it was clear. He rubbed his sore wrist and said, "You come. No more joking."

"Watch it!" Reigert cried out, raising his right hand to send a black plastic snake flying out.

Too smart to fall for the same trick twice, Carnero contemptuously let the snake bounce off his chest. He then waved the barrel of the pistol toward Bill. "Maybe I shoot your arms off so you don't do that trick again."

All of a sudden, from out of nowhere, an eighty-pound canine arrow struck the enormous bodyguard to the ground.

"What the heck!?" cried Bill.

"Our savior!" yelled Jackie. She then looked around and confirmed what she had suspected for several moments. In their meanderings down the dark University District streets, they had ended up at the corner of Clement and Chestnut streets, a hop, skip, and a jump from the Cooks' house.

Little Isaac came running up. "Holey moley, Ms. Walsh! Are you all right?"

"Yes, Isaac!" Jackie responded gratefully. "Thanks to you and Jake."

"Wow! Good thing I decided to take Jake out for a walk just now. Isn't it?"

"It sure is," Jackie confirmed, tousling the young boy's hair. "Your mom and dad get home yet?"

"Nah. They usually get a ride with that old dean guy. He doesn't let them come home until everyone else goes home and they help him empty the ashtrays and stuff."

"Okay," Jackie decided. "You go home and lock yourself in."

"What about this man?" Isaac asked, pointing to the prone Carnero.

"He'll be all right," Jackie responded. A look to Bill Reigert, who now had Carnero under guard, confirmed it. "When you go home I want you to call the Palmer University Police Precinct. Leave a message for Lieutenant Michael McGowan in the Homicide Division. He probably won't be there but insist they take down this message. Tell them Jackie Walsh and William Reigert are going to the Goodwillie mansion to talk to Mr. Goodwillie at his request. Tell the police that we are going willingly but that Mr. Goodwillie's manservant tried to make us go with him by threatening us with a gun. Tell the police they don't have to do anything but I want them to know where we are in case anything else happens. Can you remember all that?"

"What? I mean, sure," Isaac enthused. "Just one more thing. Am I taking back Jake?"

Jackie looked to her loyal Alsatian, her Dog-tor Watson as it were, and a distinct spark of mistress-dog communication passed between them. "No, Isaac," Jackie responded. "From this point on, Jake stays with me."

CHAPTER 10

When the doors to Stuart Goodwillie's trophy room burst open, the elderly bottled water baron turned without surprise to see Bill Reigert, with Jackie Walsh at his heels, push Carnero almost up to his chair.

"Good evening, Mr. Goodwillie," Reigert greeted him. He then held out Carnero's gun and presented it to the millionaire. "This belongs to your man. A crippled newsie took it away from him. I made him give it back."

Goodwillie made a face. "Oh, yes. Thank you, young man. I should be careful that the five hundred or so writers who have used that line ahead of you don't sue. Take it from one who knows, lawsuits are a pain in the—"

"Mr. Goodwillie," Jackie interrupted.

"Ms. Walsh?"

"You wanted to have a word with me?"

"I do indeed," Goodwillie responded.

"Well, if your associate," Jackie referred to the sprawled Carnero, "can roust himself I'll be happy to sit down here for a moment."

"To be sure. Where are your manners, Carnero?"

The big bodyguard stood up at once.

"As long as you're up," Goodwillie continued, "go into my study, will you? Look through the desk. See if you can find a pink slip for me that I can write something on."

The majordomo stalked out of the room and Jackie let her eyes wander over the dozens of mounted animal heads from all over the world and wondered to herself how many of those Stuart Goodwillie had actually killed.

"Not a one of those are mine, Ms. Walsh," Goodwillie informed her as if reading her mind. "I got a good price for those from an associate's widow."

"This is quite a place," Jackie remarked.

"I try to make it a home."

"It's enormous."

"Yes, when I sit in a room I don't like to look at all four walls. You are young and I am not. Let's get down to brass tacks, shall we?"

Jackie intentionally stalled the millionaire. "I wonder how much a place like this costs to run."

"You can wonder rudely about my personal business matters," Goodwillie snapped, "in the privacy of your home. That's not why I brought you here."

Jackie continued to try to keep Goodwillie off balance. "Do you ever feel guilty, Mr. Goodwillie, that you have so much and others have so little?"

"Yes," Goodwillie snarled. "I feel precisely as guilty as a gardener feels when he puts seeds in the ground and they come up as flowers, fruits, and vegetables." Goodwillie paused to wipe his mouth, then resumed. "I know the notion that a man might spend some little part of his hard-won earnings on a bit of physical comfort is abhorrent to my fellow Palmer townspeople, but you'll excuse me if I putter along in my eccentric fashion nonetheless." That being said, Goodwillie brought his hand sharply down on the copy of Dale Carnegie's best-seller that forever resided on the corner of his desk. "This nattering is to no effect, Ms. Walsh. If you're afraid I'm going to grill you about your pathetic efforts to shed some light on my dear brother's tragic slaying, you are sorely mistaken. Your efforts have been monitored and dismissed as absolutely useless!"

"What?" Jackie replied, stung. "I interviewed . . ."

"Every man jack in Palmer but the two who would actually be of any use to you." Goodwillie stepped down on a buzzer button under his desk and then turned his attention to Bill Reigert. "I'm not boring you, am I, Mr. Reigert? One does so hate to make unwelcome guests feel precisely as they should."

"Not at all, Mr. Goodwillie," Bill smiled insincerely. "I'm just glad to hear that such a distinguished town legend recognizes me."

"Don't be an ass. I receive regular reports from a detective agency. Would you like something to drink, perhaps? A glass of water?"

"Don't bother." Bill reached into an inside coat pocket and pulled out a piece of paper. He folded it into a cone. Then, as a baton appeared magically in the other hand, he used it to tap the cone once, twice, three times. A little puff of smoke obscured the cone for a moment, then when the red smoke cleared, the cone was full of water. Bill drank deeply, then offered it to Jackie. "Water?"

"No, thank you," the dark-haired film instructor replied.

"How about flowers then?" Bill offered as a bouquet sprang out of the cone instead. "No? Ah, well, then." Bill then passed a hand over the cane and the flowers withdrew inside. Clicking his fingers, Bill then snapped his wrist and the paper unrolled and was back in its original state. The magician casually showed both sides of the paper to Jackie and Goodwillie so they could see that the flowers had vanished and that the paper was dry. He then elaborately folded the paper, palmed it, turned his hand over, and then put it in his mouth as if eating it. Immediately a burst of flame came out of his mouth and Bill put a gloved hand to his mouth to stifle it. "Sorry. I guess I've got a bit of gas."

Jackie applauded politely. Goodwillie just made a face. "Oh, an illusionist, eh? Why aren't you with your fellows in the District of Columbia? Making our hard-won pennies disappear? Of course you are both too young to remember this, but there was a time when a man could make a buck in the business world. Then a bunch of red flag wavers, fuzzy-minded reformers, and mollycoddlers like that fellow Dickens riled up the great unwashed and the gutless electorate to pass a bunch of reverse slavery laws forcing an employer to pay a king's ransom to a bunch of featherbedders fast asleep on their lunch pails. Is it any wonder I've moved my pharmaceutical business to the sands of the Sahara? Is everything right with the world when I'd rather bargain with a bunch of thieving Arabs than take another bloodbath from American organized labor?

"I see my observations are falling on ignorant ears." Goodwillie then looked up to see the reentrance of his bodyguard. "Ah, Carnero. Here you are. Stop packing your suitcases with my good silver for a moment, will you, and show in Mr. Hupfelt."

Walter Hupfelt, who looked like J. Edgar Hoover blown up with a bicycle pump, appeared in the doorway. "Ready for me now, Mr. Goodwillie?"

"Why no. Not at all, Mr. Hupfelt," Goodwillie replied sarcastically. "I thought my new friends and I would play Twister for an hour, then call you. Come in and shut the door, you dim bulb! No sense air-conditioning the entire mansion, is there?"

Hupfelt stepped uneasily into the room. "Mind if I sit down, Mr. Goodwillie?"

The elderly industrialist sneered his reply. "If your knees are so weak that they can't even hold you upright, by all means. Just use some caution, Hupfelt. Those chairs are antiques, designed to hold people who could eat sensibly."

Hupfelt sat down gingerly.

Goodwillie then grimaced at his other guests and said by way of introduction, "You know Mr. Hupfelt, of course, from the university where he nominally serves as head of security. Due to the widespread practice in this town—a practice I heartily approve of, by the way—of underpaying men in responsible positions—a man willing to invest periodic infusions of capital into the right hands could have half this town in his watch pocket. And so I do. Sing like a canary, Hupfelt."

"Well, the night of the special broadcast, Mr. Goodwillie"—Hupfelt cleared his throat—"wanted me to make sure the reporter and her crew didn't get into the studio and bother his brother so . . ."

"Now we're talking about Marcella Jacobs?" clarified Jackie.

Hupfelt nodded and cleared his throat again. "The TV people had finished with Mr. Stuart Goodwillie . . ."

"Good gracious, Hupfelt. Gibbons recounted the rise and fall of the Roman Empire in the time you've taken to tell this simple story." Goodwillie then saw that Hupfelt was in some discomfort and turned even more querulous. "What's the matter, Wyatt Earp? Am I boring you? Should I put on a golden wig and sing and dance funny songs?"

Hupfelt, who had withdrawn his head to his chest for a moment, to suppress a belch, choked out, "Not at all, sir. It's just that . . ." Hupfelt paused again to clear his throat and Goodwillie erupted.

"When will we be spared your unpleasant burblings, you incompetent? Could someone be more repulsive? Do yourself a favor, man, and join a health club tomorrow. I will tell the story." Goodwillie ostentatiously stabbed his foot at the floor buzzer. "Carnero! Where are you? Sergeant Garcia here needs your services for a moment."

Carnero appeared at the door dressed in a T-shirt and sweatpants. Clearly he had not been expecting another summons. "You wanted me, sir?"

"Listen, Lurch," Goodwillie crabbed. "The immigration people won't be here to deport you until tomorrow. So make yourself useful, will you? Bring in a drink cart for my guests. Don't put anything good on it, of course. These louts wouldn't appreciate fine liquor if you spilled it on them. Right, Hupfelt? Not going too fast for you, am I?"

"Mr. Goodwillie, sir?" Carnero's voice was heard again.

"What is it, man? Has an hour gone by already? Were you planning to hit me up for yet another raise?"

"I am not going to work for you anymore, sir."

"Oh, tut, tut, Carnero," Goodwillie scoffed. "Don't start bawling. I rescind your firing. At least for the moment."

"No, sir," Carnero replied, drawing himself up. "It is I who do not wish to work for you."

"What?" Goodwillie was on his feet in a moment, pointing a bony finger between Carnero's closely set eyes. "You dare to walk out on me, sir? I'll see you hung up like a plucked chicken."

"No, sir," Carnero replied calmly. "You are finished with me. And I am finished with you. You may keep my last check. I want no more of your soiled money to touch my hands. It is tempting, sir, to tell you exactly what I think of you. But you have guests and I have no right to offend them."

Carnero bowed deeply, then straightened. "Good-bye, sir." He then pivoted on his heel and walked out.

"Can you believe it?" Goodwillie fell back amazed in his chair. "The man walks out on me in the middle of the night. No notice. No explanation. I treated that boy like an adopted son. As God is my witness, I am a veritable Job."

"Do you want me to get the drinks, Mr. Goodwillie?" Hupfelt offered.

"Keep your seat, Hupfelt!" Goodwillie barked. "You'll not get this easy an opportunity to drink yourself insensible in my liquor cabinet. *I* will get the refreshments. You earn your bank president's wages by filling in these nincompoops on what little you know." Harumphing to himself, Goodwillie left the room.

The three remaining occupants of the room looked at each other embarrassedly and then Jackie blurted out, "Walter, how could you possibly spy for a man like Stuart Goodwillie?"

Hupfelt loosened his tight collar and blushed furiously. "Never mind that. The point is this. You know that TV reporter?"

The others nodded.

"I think she may have something to do with the other Mr. Goodwillie getting it."

Goodwillie came back into the room with a bottle of white wine and a can of soda. "What are you doing? Hatching plots? Don't get cocky, people. I'll have a new bodyguard by tomorrow and I'm sure he'll be interested in impressing me by just how badly he can hurt my foes. All I'm giving you is wine. Who wants a glass of white wine?"

"I'll take one," Jackie spoke up. "Do you have a mix for it?"

Goodwillie looked dubiously at the can of soda he held in his hand. "Just this. Whatever it is. Fresca. Silly name for a soda."

"That sounds fine."

"I'd prefer red wine, myself," Bill Reigert said bravely.

Goodwillie turned to him with disdain. "Oh, would you? And how about a pair of twin geishas to rub your feet and gently strike your back with leafy twigs while you drink it? Tell you what, Julia Child, why don't I just pour you a glass of this and you can use your magical powers to turn it into whatever you like."

Goodwillie gave Jackie her drink, then held out a glass to Hupfelt. "Well, come get it, man. I'm not a barmaid."

"Actually, sir, I don't drink."

"No?" Goodwillie gave the security chief a fishy look. "That surprises me. From the looks of your gut, I'd have pegged you for a six-pack-a-day man. If you're doing this just to impress me, Hupfelt, you've failed miserably. Here. Take this soda then. All right. Are we all set? No one has to powder their elbows or make expensive long distance phone calls? Fine. The point is so simple, even you drones should grasp it. My science boys have made a study of Hupfelt's badge . . ."

Hupfelt held up his security badge with the bar-code strip on the bottom. "I had some trouble using it on the elevator slots. And when I took it out to look at it I noticed it had been cooked. I told Mr. Goodwillie and . . ."

"Please," Goodwillie interrupted. "Spare us your dreary life story, Hupfelt. The point is, I found out, with no help from any of those donut swillers in the police department, that my brother Mannheim was killed by microwaves fired from outside the room."

"Then Keith Monahan is innocent!" Jackie shouted.

"Of this particular crime, it seems," Goodwillie mumbled. "Chief Hardy and his Re-touchables have erred again—which is no surprise to this much abused taxpayer, I must say. So tomorrow, first thing, I'll have my attorney Nate Northcote go down and spring Mr. FM from protective custody."

"What about our program, Mr. Goodwillie?" Bill Reigert asked.

"Yes, well I'm sure you don't want to disappoint your dozens of listeners," Goodwillie resumed, twirling a pencil between his fingers. "I suggest you fashion your show as a tribute to my late brother. It'll add a touch of class to your little hootenanny."

"Not so fast, Mr. Goodwillie," Jackie interrupted.

"Oh, here it comes," Goodwillie groaned and addressed his next words to his dropped ceiling. "The inevitable touch. There's not a person alive, apparently, who will do a decent thing for someone else without wanting to know what's in it for them. All right. So be it. In order to have someone in this town say a decent word about the passing of one of Palmer's most beloved and distinguished citizens, Goodwillie Good Water will agree to sponsor your program."

"Better than that, Mr. Goodwillie," Jackie countered. "How about indemnifying Rodgers University for any outstanding construction costs on the Radio Arts Building?"

"What?!" Goodwillie sat up abruptly.

"Ivor Quest," Jackie explained, "is for some reason concerned that you and your brother's foundation are planning to welch on the outstanding building expenses that are still owed on the Josiah Goodwillie Radio Facility. I assured him that there couldn't possibly be any reason to worry since you and your late brother were men of your word . . ."

Goodwillie glared at the other two men, expecting some derisive look or comment.

"So," Jackie continued demurely, "if you just call the university's attorney, Mr. Holcombe, and sign whatever paper he might have for you, we'll be all set. You'll have your memorial program and you won't be out a penny you weren't planning anyway."

"Hmmm," Goodwillie responded skeptically. "What's the 'or else'?"

"It sounds to me," Jackie replied with studied negligence, "like Keith Monahan would have a heck of a lawsuit against you if he were inclined to pursue it."

Goodwillie clumsily feigned surprise. "What would I have to do with a wronged man's lawsuits against the city police department? I'm just a humble bottled water salesman!"

"Come now, Mr. Goodwillie," Jackie replied firmly.

Goodwillie settled back in his chair and half swiveled to contemplate his autographed picture of the *Enola Gay* and its crew. "Well, I could say that if Mr. Monahan were foolish enough to try to involve me in his little lawsuit, I could crush him like a gnat."

"Not if the university was behind him," Jackie replied. "The false arrest you personally insisted on, Mr. Goodwillie, brought ridicule and embarrassment to the university at a vulnerable time. I wouldn't be at all surprised if all this negative publicity hurt its recruiting efforts."

Goodwillie nodded as if approving a daring move in a game of chess. "I have nothing but respect, of course, for the legal talents of Silas Holcombe. He's one of the best, no question. Worked for F&G for many years, you know."

"Yes, I did know," Jackie responded in a quiet voice.

"Yes, I see," Goodwillie replied. "That's the way it is, then. Fine. I suppose, Ms. Walsh, you can tell your university people to send over this release, or whatever it is. If it's what you describe it to be, simply a reiteration of an agreement I've already made, then I don't see any problem with signing it."

"That'll be great, Mr. Goodwillie," Jackie smiled. "And we'll be glad to dedicate our show tomorrow night to your brother."

"What a generous offer," Goodwillie replied with genial irony. "I accept your kind tribute to Mannheim, and would like, with your kind permission, to appear briefly on your little program to read a short tribute to my late brother."

"Oh," Jackie responded, a little taken aback. "Well, I suppose we could find time somewhere . . ."

"Of course you can," Goodwillie snapped. "If the program is as entertaining as your station's previous offerings, you can take a scissors and cut at random. Slice moments off this man's routine, for instance," Goodwillie suggested, pointing his pencil at Bill Reigert. "What use is a magician on radio? It's laughable."

"That's the idea of comedy, sir," Bill replied easily.

"We'll find a place, don't worry, sir," Jackie said quickly.

"Of course you will." Goodwillie petulantly poured the rest of the wine bottle into his own glass without first offering a refill to his guest. "One other thing. Since I'm sure Ms. Jacobs and her loutish crew will want to cover this event in the same brutish fashion as she did the last, I want it made clear to the woman that she will be once again held outside the studio."

"Any particular reason, Mr. Goodwillie?" Jackie asked.

Goodwillie rose abruptly. "Make the arrangements. I'll leave the details to you. Now if you'll excuse me, at the risk of being an ungracious host, I will point out that it is nearly dawn and some of us do have a job to go to in the morning."

The others slowly clambered to their feet.

"Hupfelt," Goodwillie called out, "would you mind seeing these people out? And see if you can remember to hit the switch next to the front door on your way out. It alerts the security system not to cut you to ribbons as you leave the estate." Without so much as a good night, Goodwillie then disappeared.

Bill turned to Jackie. "What was that last part about?"

Jackie shrugged tiredly. "I'll think about it in the morning."

Hupfelt gruffly zipped up his leather jacket. "You people coming or not?"

Jackie looked around for the security camera she knew was recording their actions and said, "Whatever you're up to, Stuart Goodwillie, you'd better make sure that the murderer—whoever it is—doesn't get you this time."

CHAPTER 11

The usually grim features of the lean Palmer Police K-9 instructor creased into a happy smile as he saw the pride of his old corps enter the room.

"Alex, old boy!" Cornelius Mitchell said loudly, emphasizing every hard consonant. "How are you?"

"He's Jake now," the dog's ungreeted owner explained.

"Really?" Mitchell gave Jackie a sharp look. "You're not supposed to change a grown dog's name, you know?"

Jackie shrugged pleasantly. "He didn't seem to mind. Right, Jake?"

The long-suffering dog looked at his mistress and wagged his tail.

"What a great dog!" Mitchell enthused.

"No arguments there," Jackie smiled proudly.

"Wish we had him back," Mitchell said, not for the first time.

"Sorry," Jackie replied unrepentantly. "Jake is happily retired now."

"Oh, retired nothing," Mitchell exclaimed. "This is all our ex-chief's doing. Stillman changed Jake's age on his service records from six to ten, so he could transfer Alex to you."

"Jake," Jackie repeated.

"Jake, then!" the prematurely white-haired Mitchell replied ungraciously. "He's still in his prime, Jackie.

You had to know from the way Jake acts that he isn't any ten-year-old dog."

"Be that as it may, Con," Jackie replied. "Jake is in private practice now. Period. Didn't you want to tell me something about the dog that attacked my mother?"

Mitchell swallowed his anger and resentment and consulted a clipboard. "The dog you brought to us last week is a registered stray named 'Shag.' We talked to his former owner, Mr. Thomas Mann, and . . ."

"Excuse me," Jackie interrupted, "isn't Mr. Mann a former employee of Mel Sweeten's Dog Academy?"

"Actually," Mitchell replied, "he runs the place now. Bought it at a tax auction."

"So this dog belongs to Tom Mann?"

"He claims he sold it."

"To?"

"To Ms. Marcella Jacobs. Our local news reporter."

As Jackie very tentatively opened the door to the newsroom of KCIN, Ohio's network for "Those Who Want to Know What Their Neighbors Are Up To" in the biggest building in all of Palmer, the National Bank Tower, she waited with trepidation for someone to say, *Hey, what are you doing with that dog in here?*

However, the cynical, world-weary crew, numbering among their brethren Spike Fitzgerald, the sound man from the college radio station, just assumed the dog was part of some live commercial or the scheduled special feature on the new *Palmer Dog Academy* and didn't even look up from their racing forms. After a few moments of poking down corridors, Jackie was hailed by a nervous thirty-two-year-old news producer with slicked-back raven-colored hair and clear lens glasses worn to make his boyish face seem older.

"Hey, say. What are you doing here? Who are you?"

Jackie drew herself up, making herself taller than the young producer, and replied, "I'm here to see Marcella

Jacobs. She's expecting me."

"What's this all about? Oh, never mind. She'll tell me sooner or later, I guess. No rush. I'm just the show's producer. Maybe I can read about it in tomorrow's paper." Having tried and failed to get Jackie to feel sorry for him, the young producer pointed his finger down another corridor. "Marcella's through there." And after so saying, producer Ruben Baskette stalked off holding his stomach and talking to himself.

Jackie proceeded a little farther, then smacked herself on the forehead. "What am I doing? I have a tracking dog with me. Jake, find Marcella Jacobs."

Jackie stopped at a water fountain and when she turned around Jake was gone. "This is like the old joke," Jackie said to herself. " 'Driver, follow that cab!' and before you can get in off he goes."

"Hey!"

Jackie turned at the voice and saw that a man sitting at a desk in an open office was hailing her. Looking more closely, Jackie could see it was Drew Feigl, the gangly, beetle-browed investigative reporter whose enterprising forays against those who would pollute rain forests, squelch free speech, or deny a homeless person the right to sleep in a public library were the stuff legends are made of.

"Did you say something?" Jackie asked the reporter.

"What you just said, mind if I use it?" Feigl gave Jackie an appealing smile.

"Sure," Jackie shrugged. "But it's been done a hundred times."

"Just call me 'Mister 101,' " Feigl announced. He then wrote out a chit and held it out to Jackie. "Take this to the cashier and she'll cut you a check."

"What is this?" Jackie asked.

"A voucher. Good for one hour's pay at the standard writer's rates. You *are* a member of the writer's union, aren't you?"

Jackie nodded dumbly.

"All right, then. Excuse me!" Feigl then got up and closed his door and after a moment Jackie could hear through it, "And so to this impartial observer, the United States' policy toward Nicaragua has been like the guy who says, 'Follow that cab' and then the cab speeds off before he can ever get in. Reporting exclusively for KCIN, this is Drew Feigl, Neighborhood EyeWitness News."

As Jackie turned away she was startled to see Marcella Jacobs approaching her, being pulled by the cloth belt of her dress by a friendly German shepherd named Jake.

"Marcella!"

"Jackie! Is this your dog?"

"Man, talk about service."

Marcella tugged her dress free of Jake's mouth. Fortunately for her, the big dog let her. "I don't find this at all funny. How would you like to see yourself facing a kidnapping charge?"

"I didn't tell Jake to bring you," Jackie said innocently. "That was his idea. And you can't bring kidnapping charges against a dog."

"Oh, no?"

"No, Marcella," Vic Kingston, the craggy news anchor, said as he passed them carrying a large cup of coffee. "It is after all the *Mann* Act."

Detesting any witticism that she had not herself uttered, Marcella stamped her foot, eliciting a warning growl from Jake, and demanded, "What do you want from me?"

"Just a few seconds, Marcella," Jackie replied.

"My agent tells me I make a hundred and sixty dollars a second. You sure you can afford it?"

Jackie sighed. She and Marcella had been friends at one point, but Marcella's demotion from the Palmer *Chronicle* to KCIN (both newspaper and television station were owned by the same communications company, Ming Enterprises) and her promotion from fact check-

er and rough copywriter to on-camera personality had
made her drop her old friends like so many not-so-hot
potatoes.

"Marcella," Jackie tried to explain, knowing that she
had an unreceptive audience, "I'm not paying for your
on-camera presence. I'm simply here to give you a tip
on the story."

"Call my secretary," Marcella snapped, swiveling to
go.

"It involves you personally, Marcella," Jackie said
loudly.

Marcella turned. "How so?"

"Stuart Goodwillie has been investigating your past."

"Me?" Marcella replied, genuinely astonished. "I
thought he had railroaded your pal Keith Monahan
into the gas and electric chair."

"He's found a better suspect. You."

"Me?!" Marcella at once reached for a cigarette.

"Marcella, Stuart Goodwillie has had people go
through his brother's papers. They've found out that
Mannheim Goodwillie used his power to get you fired.
First in Florida, then in Philadelphia. He wanted you
to have to come back here to Palmer in disgrace. And
when Mannheim saw you had turned your setback into
a success here, there was a strong suspicion he would
have tried to ruin you again."

Marcella looked around. Knowing ears and eyes everywhere were trained on their conversation, she forced out
a transparent lie. "I . . . I don't know what you're talking
about."

"Well, you can debate the point with Mr. Goodwillie
if you like. He apparently bought some tapes that were
made at the time which included a conversation between
you and Mannheim. Threats were made."

"I was just . . ." Marcella then realized that she had
been tricked into admitting something and clenched her
jaw.

Jackie waited a moment, then resumed. "Stuart Goodwillie is planning to make an announcement on the *Golden Biscuit Radio Hour* tonight. He hasn't said what's in his statement, but I strongly suspect it's going to name you directly. If I were you, I'd be there tonight."

"Oh, no!" Marcella protested quickly.

"Oh, yes, you will!" yelled Ruben Baskette, emerging at once from his producer's office, where he had been listening in on the intercom.

"Hey, if you don't want the assignment, I'll be glad to go!" yelled Drew Feigl, who had obviously been listening with his ear pressed to the other side of his closed door.

"Oh, go along why don't you?" cried Vic Kingston, the anchorman who had ducked into the next corridor to eavesdrop. "I'll be happy to read your story tonight. Just give me the script."

Leaving the trapped Marcella to deal with her helpful, loyal colleagues, Jackie put her leash back on Jake and said, "Eight o'clock tonight. Come early if you want a good seat."

All of a sudden, a scream cut through the clamor. All heads turned and a pale-faced secretary stumbled out into the corridor from one of the editing suites. "Something's happened!" she said hollowly.

"What?" cried Ruben.

Jackie, Jake, and the three reporters all went to see for themselves.

Pushing their way into the suite, they saw Spike Fitzgerald lying on one of the Steenbeck sound consoles, obviously quite dead. His headphones lay next to him and Jackie, moving quickly, upended a coffeepot on his murderer.

"What is it?" Kingston asked, searching for his glasses.

"Looks like a black spider," cried Feigl.

Jackie left the trapped creature to the inquisitive

Feigl—he was obviously good with bugs—and walked over to hug the shaking, pale Marcella.

"Who is doing this, Jackie?" she asked.

"I don't know, Marcella," Jackie replied. "But now we know for sure that it isn't Keith Monahan."

CHAPTER 12

Keith Monahan, taking advantage of the musical break, grabbed another rubber microphone saliva guard out of the box and exchanged it for the one he had used for the riotous first half of the *Golden Biscuit Radio Hour*. The red light came up. Keith put his tinted glasses back on and beamed out into the lights, allowing the studio audience to hear him, while simultaneously thumbing up the on lever on his mike.

"Hello, happy listeners, and welcome back to the second serving with butter and jelly of the *Golden Biscuit Radio Hour*. The first half of tonight's show was dedicated to that great radio comedian, Jack Benny. Here in the last thirty minutes—we may run over a bit into the *Christic Society*'s time tonight—we do our usual schtick; including 'Bill and Lil, Radio Magicians.' " Keith nodded and the lights on him faded and came up on Bill Reigert and his lovely twin sister, Lil, sitting on stools in PS1, holding only microphones.

"Hello, Bill!"

"Greetings, Lil. Goodness gracious, sister, if the folks at home saw how little you were wearing the FCC would saw us in half."

"They'd make us disappear, anyway. Tee hee."

"Ladies and gentlemen, and anyone else who's listening, my sister and I are," Bill lowered his voice impressively, "*illusionists*. Keep that in mind tonight

when in hearing with your mind's eye, you think you
see . . ."

"Son of a gun!" Monahan yelled in an "average Joe"
voice. "Where'd that fiery sword come from?"

"*Ach, Gott im Himmel,*" Marcus Baghorn kvetched
next. "A tiger with an unfriendly expression on its puss."

"Oh, my goodness," Lil bawled out.

"What is it?" Monahan asked.

"I'm floating. I'm floating straight up in the air!"

"Amazing, isn't it?" Bill commented. "But illusion is
as old as time itself."

"Wow, Bill!" Lil enthused. "What a beautiful swirling
globe of energy!"

"Watch it change, Lil!"

"Stand back, everyone!" Lil called out. "That flame
must go twenty feet in the air!"

"That's great, Lil," Bill responded. "Because I sure
am hungry."

"Oh, Bill! Are you really going to eat the whole
thing?"

"I sure am," Bill replied.

"Goodness! Well, he looks like he knows what he's
doing," Lil continued bravely, a quaver in her voice.
"But does anyone have an antacid? I'm sure he'll need
it when he gets done."

Bill made a gulping sound.

"Bill, are you all right?"

"Fine and dandy, Lil," Bill replied to a timed sound
effect (of a flame burning). "Oops, sorry, sir. I'm sure
those eyebrows will grow back in time. Urp."

"Bill!" Lil protested.

"Sorry. And sorry about my breath. Do you have a
Certs with that golden drop of Retsyn, Lil?"

"No."

"Well, don't worry. We should get a case after that
commercial plug."

"Oh, you're terrible."

"No, I'm Bill."

"And I'm Lil."

"And we're the TWIN . . . Radio Magicians! See you next time, folks!"

Monahan struck the appropriate magical disappearing tone on his xylophone and then resumed, "Bill and Lil, Radio Magicians, who remind you that bad magic isn't magic at all." Monahan struck another tone. "And now we come to a more somber segment. As you know if you've been listening from the top of the program, our show tonight has been dedicated to Spike Fitzgerald, a technician who worked with us for many years, and Mr. Mannheim Goodwillie, the late great philanthropist. Mannheim Goodwillie's story is one of courage and dedication. At the age of nineteen, just out of Francis of Assissi College here in Palmer, Mannheim courageously took a vice president's job that he was in no way capable of handling in his father's multimillion-dollar company and somehow managed not to muck things up. I'm talking about a man almost as widely recognized in our beautiful city of Palmer as the man in the toilet bowl who sold their biggest selling product in a series of brilliant television commercials . . ." Darting a quick look over to see how the dead man's millionaire brother was taking it, Monahan swung into the cue, "And now I'll let you hear directly from the man who washed our water, if not our minds, Stuart Goodwillie."

Almost as nettled as Monahan intended him to be, Stuart Goodwillie, clutching his five-by-nine index cards, blinked hard as the red light came on, then went into his prepared remarks. "Thank you, Mr. Monahan. Clearly a sojourn in jail hasn't impaired your ability to get everything precisely wrong. Folks, I come to you tonight not to ask you to buy my bottled water, Goodwillie Good Water, the only *safe* choice in Palmer, which this week features a special discount—when you purchase the three-liter bottle at the regular price we'll give you a second three-liter bottle for only ninety-four cents. A once a year sale you might say.

"Beyond that, I come before you tonight, neighbors, with a quiet word of warning about our very own radical fruitcake television station, KCIN, 'Voice of the Lefties.' Of course if they had their way, none of us would have radios at all—just thin, grimy copies of the Palmer *Pravda*, the official party organ. Can you see it? At night we'd be frog-marched to public televisions where we'd watch Comrade Marcella lead us in choral arrangements of 'The Internationale' and other peasant labor ballads.

"No, my close, dear friends, I come to you on this sad occasion because KCIN has graduated from showcasing nincompoops to murderers. I refer to the muckraking scion of the Unfriendly Witness News Hour, *Miz* Marcella Jacobs. Since it would be pointless to hold up a picture, I'll play you twenty seconds of her odious voice."

Monahan cued Sylvie Thompson to roll the Marcella Jacobs tape.

"Is there a Republican Party Terrorist Cabal responsible for testing laser rays from space and making us think it's just a nasty sunburn . . . ?"

Goodwillie's voice returned. "Like scraping paint off a car trunk, isn't it? Last week at this time my brother Mannheim was sitting not ten feet from where I'm standing tonight. The occasion was, as you may remember, the opening of this radio station's Josiah Goodwillie Radio Facility. Mannheim was here in this studio telling a few heartwarming tales about how my father started his business with just a handful of herbs and a big piece of cheesecloth, when all of a sudden, the KCIN commando team, quarterbacked by the mannish Ms. Jacobs, burst in. The valiant security team, led by Dominican Republic war hero 'Big Walt' Hupfelt, held them back the best they could. Of course the insolent Jacobs had been banned from the interview for medical and humanitarian reasons. My brother Mannheim had a bad heart and too much excitement, he knew, would cause white-hot daggers of cardiac pain to tear him apart like a biscuit . . ."

"A golden biscuit," Monahan couldn't help adding.

Goodwillie looked over, ruminated a moment about how much it would cost him to have the usual assassins garrote the fleshy radio announcer in a dark alley, then returned to his copy. "And so they gave the fateful order. I have here on a tape, which fortunately wandered into my hands, a quote from the ambitious Ms. Jacobs speaking to her incompetent union sound man."

The familiar voice of Marcella Jacobs said, "Crank it up, Jock. I don't want to miss a word . . ."

Then the sample phrase of Marcella's voice played earlier was played again. "Is there a Republican Party Terrorist Cabal . . . ?"

"Sounds about the same, doesn't it?" Goodwillie asked disingenuously. "I'm not a doctor, folks. But if I were I'd tell you that medical evidence shows that my brother Mannheim was killed by microwaves hurled into the ozone by the odious assassins at KCIN. What to do about all this? Six hundred years ago an English king named Henry said, 'Is there no one here who will rid me of this mad priest?' I say to you now, as Palmer's richest citizen, 'Is there no one in this town who will rid me of this enterprising newswoman-slash-murderess?' "

The voice tape ran again. "This is Marcella Jacobs, for KCIN TV."

"I'll make it worth your while," Goodwillie hissed.

"And now," Monahan resumed, "here's Jovial Jerry Anderson and the Rhythm Polka boys singing 'Gosh O' Golly Gee' . . ."

Not five minutes after the broadcast ended, Jackie burst into Keith Monahan's office and accosted the half-clad radio instructor. "What the heck do you think you're doing?"

"I was about to change my pants," Monahan responded. "But I can wait."

"Save your wisecracks for your comedy shows," Jackie responded angrily. "I mean what are you doing letting that lunatic Goodwillie come on the air and put out a call for bounty hunters?! Believe it or not, Keith, there hasn't been a jury trial yet. It may turn out that Marcella Jacobs had nothing to do with the microwaves that killed Mannheim Goodwillie."

"What can I tell you, Jackie?" Monahan said flatly. "You were the one who negotiated his coming on the show. He wouldn't let me know ahead of time and I couldn't very well cut in and censor him."

"Why not?" Jackie demanded. "They do it to some radio personalities all the time."

"Jackie," Monahan protested. "I don't know why you're so surprised. You worked for television. They have the same saying there. 'You pay the freight, you pull the weight.'"

"But to kowtow to the devil, Keith!?"

"Come on now."

Jackie was really getting worked up. "He is the president/dictator that Sinclair Lewis prophesied in *It Can't Happen Here*."

"Please," Stuart Goodwillie protested, coming out of Monahan's bathroom. "All this flattery is turning my head."

"Why didn't you tell me he was here?" Jackie raged.

"You didn't give me a chance!" Monahan yelled back.

"I'm going to go after Marcella!" Jackie announced. "And try to bring her back here. And you'd better hope I catch up to her before one hair on her head is harmed."

"Oh, by all means," Goodwillie simpered. "Our prayers go with you, Ms. Walsh, as you undertake your compassionate quest to help the clearly guilty. No greater love hath no woman and so on . . ."

Jackie stormed out of the office, slamming the door.

She stalked past Evan Stillman, Stuart Goodwillie's new security chief, cracking, "One side, Faust," and then proceeded out to her Jeep.

"Jake!" she called out. The big dog materialized from whatever section of the narrow, shrub-lined faculty parking lot he had been investigating and hopped in through the open driver's side door.

Jackie sat down, strapped in, and turned to her partner. "Jake. This is the hardest thing I ever asked you. Smell this." Jackie held up a handkerchief that Marcella Jacobs had dropped in her propitious flight through the lobby. "Marcella wears a lot of perfume and likes to drive with her windows open. Do you think you can track her?"

The big dog at once wagged its tail.

"Good dog, Jake!" Jackie exulted. And with a hearty "Let's go!" she threw the Jeep into reverse.

As they motored toward Wardville with both windows open, Jake guided Jackie with a series of barks onto the Henderson Interstate.

"I know it's tough, boy, but keep trying," Jackie urged, yelling above the four-lane traffic. Then, feeling around behind her for a moment, the dark-haired film instructor came up with a sack of groceries she had purchased before going to the radio station. What could she come up with? A carrot. No. Jake liked vegetables at times but it was clear that this was a job for meat. Jackie's next try in the grab bag yielded a Spicy Pete Meat Stick. Perfect. The things hadn't killed Peter yet, thank God, and if Spicy Petes weren't meat they were the next best thing. Jackie pounded the Pete on her knee and the spicy meat rod oozed its way up out of the top of the package. After a nod that it was okay, Jake hopped on the treat like the big dog that he was.

As Jackie finally watched her dog suck down the greasy meat munch with barely a chew, she remembered sadly a rare happy time with her ex-husband Cooper when they had gone necking in his little white Volkswagen bug and he lit a Spicy Pete with a lighter so they'd have a night light. It had burned longer, it seemed, than their love.

"Okay, boy!" Jackie jerked herself back to reality by slapping her dog playfully on the side. "Back to work!"

A signal from Jake to take the Perez Place exit to the north end of Palmer caused Jackie to vaguely remember that Marcella now lived here in a northside neighborhood. A few moments later they pulled up just behind Marcella's car. Recovering from the surprise of stumbling over her quarry so suddenly, Jackie furiously honked the horn and waved frantically. She signaled Marcella to pull over so they could have a talk. Marcella and Jackie met each other on the road halfway between the two cars.

"What the hell do you want?" screamed Marcella.

"I'm trying to save your neck!" Jackie yelled back at her.

"What do you call this, Jackie?!" the angry news-woman demanded. "Are you luring me out into the street so some sniper can pick me off?"

"Marcella!" Jackie said firmly. "I know you had nothing to do with Mannheim Goodwillie's murder."

"Oh, great!" Marcella shouted, although a little less angry. "*Now* you say it. A little earlier tonight on radio before ten or twenty thousand people would have been a better time, don't you think?"

"I had nothing to do with writing that Stuart Goodwillie spot," Jackie replied loudly.

"No, maybe not, but I didn't hear you making any flying tackles either!" Marcella's eyes flashed. She was just hopping mad. "Even after it was loud and clear what Stuart Goodwillie was going to do, nobody interrupted or cut him off. Where were you? Backstage, knitting a noose?"

"That's enough!" Jackie shouted, grabbing Marcella by the arms.

Marcella easily slipped out of Jackie's hands. "You

let go of me. You don't fool me. You've hated me and have been out to get me since I became more successful than you. And just because I've dated Michael a few times!"

"Would you stop it?!" Jackie practically shrieked. "I know who the murderer is and I'm inviting you to go with me now and uncover him. That's a pretty good story, don't you think? Now, are you interested?"

"Yes!" Marcella yelled without thinking. "I mean, of course. Where are we going?"

Jackie's mind flitted to another matter. "You dated Michael, hunh?"

Marcella flipped her hair and climbed into the driver's side of Jackie's Jeep. "Let's go. I'm ready when you are."

CHAPTER 13

Jackie and Marcella didn't immediately go to confront the man Jackie believed to be the murderer. First they made a stop.

Michael McGowan, an honest policeman who paid more than half his take-home salary each week in alimony, lived on Ash Street, near Broadway in an old, narrow pre-war building. McGowan's small studio was on the second floor. He had a shower stall in his tiny kitchenette, a living-room set that was composed of two comfortable lounger chairs, a large teardrop-shaped coffee table that doubled as a dinner table, and a big old secondhand horsehair couch. The bedroom area of the apartment consisted of a tall bureau that was McGowan's only closet space, a large platform bed, and a water closet. Jackie hadn't intended to catch McGowan in bed. She certainly hadn't intended to find her friend Sylvia Brown there too.

When the door opened and the overhead light came on, Michael sat straight up in bed. "What the . . . ?"

"Sorry, Michael," Jackie said quickly, turning and flicking off the light. She threw something on the counter before exiting. "Just returning your key."

Although Marcella had much longer legs than Jackie, the dark-haired film instructor matched her stride for stride as they stalked down the hall.

"Jerk," she enunciated.

"Yeah, well, aren't they all?" Marcella responded.

"I guess it's time for me to find out," said Jackie.

"Any prospects?"

"Oh, yeah."

"Well?"

Jackie started down the fire stairs to the ground floor. "Let's talk murder, Marcella."

"I don't know, Jackie," the newswoman hesitated. "Remember he has a gun and that broad he was with had muscles to spare."

"Not McGowan, Marcella. Mannheim Goodwillie!"

"Oh, him."

"It's time we bearded the murderer in his own den."

Marcella liked the sound of it but had to ask, "We're going there now?"

Jackie shook her head as she held the stairway door for Marcella. "We still need some muscle. And I've got an idea for that."

The two women straight-armed the apartment building front doors, a bit that looked impressive as heck but immediately caused the doors to come right back at them.

"Ow!"

"Are you all right?"

Jackie held the Jeep's passenger side door open for her newfound friend as Marcella rubbed her sore elbow. "I think you're right about getting that extra muscle, Jackie. I talk a good game but I can't fight for . . ."

All of a sudden a voice rang out, "Jackie!"

Jackie looked up and saw a half-dressed McGowan calling down to her from his window. "Will you wait a minute?! Can we talk?"

"Sure, we can talk," Jackie mumbled, mostly to herself. "Good-bye, Michael."

While Marcella stayed in the double-parked Jeep in case they had to move it, Jackie strode straight up to the only licensed vendor in the Palmer Jay Cees Park brave enough to stay open after dark.

"Lemon ice?" the vendor asked.

"I've got a better proposition for you," Jackie responded.

Primo Melendez Carnero, looking very distinguished in the white coverall uniform the town of Palmer insisted its downtown vendors wear, drew himself up proudly. "If you have arrived on behalf of Mr. Goodwillie, you come here in vain . . ."

Jackie felt a spasm of annoyance pass through her. Why hadn't she taken the lemon ice when Carnero had first offered it? Now she'd have to wait until the big vendor finished his spiel.

"I worked hard and saved many years for this truck. This is what I do now. Not break legs. I sell sugary cold things that make people happy and I am now content with what I do."

Jackie held out a couple of folded bills. "We'll offer you two hundred dollars for a night's work."

"Give me a minute, I just have to lock up."

As the intrepid foursome sped to their destination they all had a lemon ice. Even Jake.

Carnero seemed a little worried about the big dog next to him who hadn't been any too friendly when they had first met on a hill overlooking the Palmer reservoir outside of town. "Are you sure that it's all right I feed this dog?"

"Sure," Jackie remarked. "Just one word of warning, though. He really hates it when you stop."

Marcella watched Carnero start to frantically search through his pockets for additional treats and screamed with laughter. "I love that one. Who is it? Jack Benny?"

"Bob Newhart," Jackie replied, sucking a little lemon juice off her arm.

As they sped along, Marcella asked just a wee bit

worriedly, "Are you sure you don't want me to hold your cup while you drive?"

"Not to worry." Jackie flipped the almost finished ice toward the backseat. Jake caught it cleanly in his mouth, neatly placed his own vacuumed-clean paper neatly in the garbage sack, and then started in happily on his new treat.

"Besides," Jackie continued, "if there's one thing I can do in this world, it's drive. I once changed from a formal funeral dress to a skindiving suit while behind the wheel."

"Wow!" exclaimed Marcella, impressed but not really reassured.

"As you can imagine the hardest part is changing from the high heels to the flippers."

Carnero, this time in on the joke, laughed harder than anyone.

Suddenly they had arrived.

"The Palmer Dog Academy?" Marcella asked.

Jackie nodded. She didn't tell the others the dream she had had the night before.

In Jackie's nightmare the residence still had the sign "Mel Sweeten's Dog Academy" outside. Jackie had been walking through the grounds for some reason, perhaps looking for Jake. She had wandered back by the kennels and had heard voices. Jackie had relaxed when she realized it was just the radio, old-time radio show tapes and Rush Limbaugh recordings that the Sweetens had played throughout the grounds to drive out groundhogs. Then she saw it. A woman strangling a man. It was Sylvia Brown, dressed like Ice of the "American Gladiators," and her victim was Michael.

Even before tonight, when she had seen the evidence with her own eyes, Jackie had known there was something going on between those two. In her dream Jackie had run up to help the poor policeman when all of a sudden he had turned to her and said, "No! Everything's fine, Jackie. I like it."

Jackie had awoken in a pool of sweat.

"Jackie."

"Hunh!"

"Why are we here?" Marcella asked. "Is this something to do with Jake?"

Jackie shook her head once to clear it. Man, those lemon ices were murder. "No, Marcella. This involves Thomas Mann."

"The German mystical writer?" The newswoman's eyes flashed in outrage. "What, are you kidding? This isn't *Death in Venice*, Jackie. This is *Death in Palmer*. Two people are dead, Jackie. I may be next—if Goodwillie's vigilantes get ahold of me. Or if I get thrown in the Palmer jail. You may not remember, but my stories are responsible for a lot of people being there."

"No, Marcella. This is another Thomas Mann."

"Come on, Jackie."

Carnero and Jake grew a little bit restive on the backseat.

"I can't believe," Marcella continued, "that a mother would risk years of ridicule by naming her son Thomas Mann. Especially in a German-American town like Palmer."

"Neither can I," Jackie answered, pulling on the lever opening her car door.

Jackie shushed the others as they poured out of the Jeep; then, as they made their way quietly to the front gate, the dark-haired film instructor continued her explanation. "I met Tom Mann, who used to work here when the Sweetens owned the place. I noticed his strange name and thought about asking him about it, but of course . . ."

"You had murders to solve," Marcella filled in. "Go on."

"Later," Jackie continued, "I thought about it and thought he had shortened it from something embarrassing, or maybe a longer German name."

"Like 'Mannheim,' " Marcella guessed quickly. "There's a relation?"

"In a way." Jackie turned to Carnero as they neared the gate. "Primo, you know Tom Mann the dog handler, don't you?"

"Yes," Carnero nodded. "He was Mr. Mannheim's ward."

"You hear?" Jackie asked.

Marcella reached for her recorder.

"Mannheim Goodwillie almost married Mann's mother," Jackie related. "They broke up and Jane Bellamy stole Mannheim away from Tom's mother, Manfredda. But the old man stayed fond of the boy. He helped him along. After the big fight with Henry Obermaier, young Tom ended up not going to college at all. By the time our mayor had dropped both Goodwillies for their family doctor and Mannheim went back to his wife, Manfredda was ill. Breast cancer. She died twelve years ago. Shortly before she died, Thomas Marland Kruegar changed his name to Mann to honor his would-be stepfather. Mannheim probably helped him from time to time, but Thomas was a proud young man and never took much from his benefactor. I'll bet, however, that he knew Mannheim had left him a sizable sum in his will. Mannheim didn't have many friends, after all. His wife is in bad shape. She had a stroke ten years ago and resides in a quality care home outside of Palmer. Mannheim's brother is wealthy. He doesn't need his brother's money and besides they quarreled many years ago. So my guess is Thomas was set to inherit *something*—at least in the five figures. The bulk of the estate and Mannheim's share of the family business would go to his son, Arthur, of course. But Arthur died several months ago in a car accident—although everyone agrees that he was an obsessively safe driver."

"It just goes to show how unfair life is," Marcella

interrupted, unable to resist the joke. "Safe drivers like Arthur Goodwillie die in fiery infernos while reckless drivers motoring down the highway at a hundred miles an hour while eating popsicles . . ."

Jackie laughed, then addressed the big South American vendor and ordered him, "Carnero, if this woman interrupts me again, snap her neck like a matchstick."

Carnero "ho, ho, ho'd" at the uncanny impression of his former employer.

"Anyway, to wrap this all up," Jackie continued. "Mann saw an opportunity—I don't know whether he had anything to do with Arthur Goodwillie's death or not—as things stand now, I would vote yes. Mann realized that he now stood to inherit a great deal more than before. If Mannheim died before making a new will, then the money which would have gone to Arthur would be divided by the others. Already this means millions to Tom Mann—and if anything should by chance happen to Mannheim's comatose wife, why then . . ."

"This is incredible," Marcella commented as she flipped over the tape in her recorder. "Where did you get this stuff?"

"Well, a lot of background comes from Jean Scott, my mother's friend who works as a reviewer on the *Chronicle*. She dug this stuff out for me. Your friend Stuart Allen at the *Chronicle* was also helpful."

"Good old Bingo!" Marcella beamed, remembering her favorite fellow workmate fondly. "He's still the one I call when I want to know what's really going on in the world. TV news is all a big con game, Jackie."

The film instructor nodded. "Anyway, the first time I started thinking about Tom Mann was when Con Mitchell at the police department told me that he had trained the dog which had tried to break into my mother's house. He told the police that he had sold the dog to you."

"And you didn't call me to check?" Marcella asked indignantly.

"I didn't have to," Jackie replied impatiently. "I've been to your apartment, remember. I know your landlord doesn't allow pets."

"That's right!"

"Then I talked to Ron Dunn, last night and this morning. And he told me that what happened to Mannheim Goodwillie is the same thing that happened to one of the characters in the *I Love a Mystery* episode he did many years ago."

"Jackie!" Marcella exclaimed. "Last night and this morning? You spent the night with Ronald Dunn?"

"Well," Jackie grinned. "After I dropped off Bill Reigert I realized that I had stranded Ron and that he still needed a ride back to his Lamborghini and one thing led to another and . . ."

"And?"

"This is strictly not for publication. Understand?"

"I wouldn't dream . . ." Marcella protested.

"I don't believe you," Jackie said at once. "Anyway, I asked again in the green room before the show tonight and Yelena Gruber mentioned that she auditioned for an *I Love a Mystery* from the same period, whose plot involved a radio sound man being killed by a black widow spider. Apparently you can tap an area between the thorax and abdomen on a spider's back with a hard pencil-shaped piece of ice, evoking a temporary paralysis that lasts several hours, giving you time to carefully place . . ."

"Jackie!" Marcella exclaimed. "Are you saying Tom Mann wrote for this old radio show?"

"No." Jackie shook her head impatiently. "He would have had to be my dad's age." A spasm of sadness shot through Jackie, as it always did when she realized her father was no longer alive. "He was a fan, I'd guess. Maybe he taped the shows on an old reel to reel or kept a diary relating the plots as he listened to them. Carnero, do you know if Mannheim Goodwillie liked the *I Love a Mystery* show?"

Carnero nodded at once. "My older brother worked for the Goodwillies then. That was Mr. Mannheim's favorite radio program."

"So Mann killed Mannheim in a way he thought his 'uncle' might appreciate. I don't know if the young Thomas hated his 'uncle' for not marrying his mother or whether he just got tired of waiting for his inheritance."

"I bet a place like this isn't cheap to run," Marcella commented.

"Good point," Jackie agreed. "Well, I'm tired of standing here talking. What about the rest of you?"

Carnero and Jake immediately showed their eagerness to proceed.

Jackie tried the gate and saw it was held closed with a sturdy-looking padlock. "Locked," she said.

"You didn't call ahead to let Mr. Mann know we were coming?" Marcella asked in mock amazement.

"No," Jackie replied with a certain tone of finality. "How about it, Carnero? Know anything about locks?"

The big man nodded, making the silver pesos on the hatband of his gaucho hat clink merrily. "Almost as much as I know about making lemon ices," Carnero replied with a significant pause.

Jackie and Marcella, both having been in show business long enough to recognize a cue when they heard one, rushed in with a—

"And a wonderful pair of ices they were too!"

"Tangy without being tart!"

"Palmer's refreshing new taste treat at the oh-so-affordable price," Marcella concluded professionally.

Carnero nodded, satisfied to hear those few precious words of approbation that let an artist know his work was good. Without further ado he reached inside his sports jacket and pulled out a gleaming silver cold chisel about six inches in length.

Jackie noted with approval that Carnero was wearing a bulletproof Kevlar vest beneath his coat.

Carnero placed the tip of the cold chisel in the lock, twisted until drops of sweat appeared on his massive brow, then grunted as the lock snapped open and fell broken to the ground.

"Thew!" he expectorated. "You can tell that lock was not made in my country where it would have taken two strong men and a chisel three times as big to open it."

This sounded a little Munchausen to Jackie but she let it slide and threw open the gate. Two small guard dogs immediately ran up. The first, a terrier like Toto in the Oz series, was made short work of. Jake feinted low as if going for a front leg, then came up high and grabbed the small dog up in the air. Carnero slipped the chisel in the dog's mouth and wrapped his jacket over it and then threw dog and coat over the fence into some bushes.

Jackie distracted the second dog, a mongrel chow, with a Spicy Pete stick. When the small dog stopped to scarf down the greasy treat, Jake came over and sat on him. Dazed and demoralized, the dog was easily scooped up and dumped over the fence into a locked run by Carnero.

Then, with Jackie in the lead, the quartet made its way toward the main building. The dark-haired film instructor didn't know whether the dog trainer was armed or what microwaves would do to three people and a dog who didn't have pacemakers, but she proceeded cautiously. Eventually they reached the back door.

Jackie looked in the rearmost dog run and saw the fat, stupid-looking Raphael, a beagle of uncertain ancestry whom Mel Sweeten had once palmed off on another dog owner, the current head of the Canine Rights Lobby, Thalia Gilmore, telling her it

was the pup of beagle champions, Dartagnan's Finest
Hour and Nightingale of the Forest, colloquially known
as Fred and Karen.

Raphael did not raise a fuss because he was happily
listening to records of the old radio program *I Love a
Mystery.*

Jackie carefully opened the red-painted screen door
and then cautiously tried the inner door's knob. "It's
open," she whispered.

The others carefully followed Jackie into the kitchen
of the house as the radio voice of Lyle Talbot (the
program was also airing inside the house) was heard
to say, "Hold it right there, Tom. We've got you dead
to rights."

Tom Mann, a large, red-faced man with fat, freckled
arms and beefy fists, sat at the table with a half-empty
plastic iced tea pitcher full of ice, water, bourbon, and
non-alcohol beer. When he saw that he had guests, the
big man reached over and turned off his tape recorder
with a loud snap.

"Right on cue," Mann said in his strange, high-
pitched, cracking Andy Devine voice. "Anyone want
a diet boilermaker?"

Marcella flicked on her tape recorder and Jackie
approached.

"Hello, Tom."

"Jackie! Long time no see. You too, Jake. How are
you?" He held his hand out as if to pat Jake on the snout,
but the police dog refused this bribe of affection. "And
I recognize you, Miss Jacobs. You know, if I wasn't so
crocked, I could do something violent and make Stuart
Goodwillie a happy man."

"Don't even try," Jackie warned him.

Mann looked blearily up at the Kevlar-vest-clad
Carnero holding a heavy Colt .45 pistol on him.

"And of course I recognize Señor Primo. You're like
me, Carnero. You hang around those people all those

years and what did you get for all your troubles? A kick in the teeth, just like yours truly. You should be on my side, not theirs. What are they paying you, pal? I'll double it."

Carnero slowly shook his head. "I remember you too, sir. I never trusted you. Not for a moment."

Mann laughed ironically. "Can you see why I didn't hesitate to murder? Why would I fear public condemnation? People have hated me all my life. Tom, Tom, the dog-show man. Teaching dogs to stifle their better instincts and not poop all over the floors of masters unworthy of their respect."

"So you admit killing Mannheim Goodwillie," Marcella enunciated for posterity. "And Jesse 'Spike' Fitzgerald, as well."

"Oh, yes. Yes," Mann said clearly, obviously only too willing to have his confession down on tape. "When you've trained dogs all your life, spiders are a snap. Arachnids are so much smarter than mammals. Including us, I'm afraid. Some day they'll rule us all."

"You act as if you've been expecting us, Tom," Jackie pointed out.

"Oh, yes. I knew you were on to me when I heard you'd written that Jack Benny thing. A perfect way to taunt me." Mann raised his jelly glass in an ironic toast. "I salute you."

"What do you mean?" asked Marcella.

"Jack Benny and Rochester. Mannheim Goodwillie and little Tommy Kruegar. I always thought they cast Eddie Anderson regardless of the fact he was black. The big uneducated guy, good with his hands, has always worked for the smart-mouthed rich guy since the beginning of time. When I didn't go to college, Mr. Mannheim used to call me in to do odd jobs. He didn't have dogs to train, so he'd have me planing down doors and repainting his car. Oh, I didn't *have* to do these things, but if I didn't, well then, who knows what might happen to the legacy he might have left me? I didn't have a life of my own until his wife had her stroke and he moved to Florida."

"That's when you started working for the Sweetens?" Jackie asked.

"Sure, Mel and I were in the Elks Club together." Mann took another sip of his drink with a great smacking of lips and then continued, "He hired me to help out here. We weren't close, exactly, but he was pretty much the only pal I had. He gave me a job when nobody else would. I never stopped being grateful to him for that."

"Even when you helped kill him?" Jackie asked quietly.

"Absolutely," Mann nodded. "Hey, I still feel guilty about that."

"I knew something was fishy," Jackie said. "When you disappeared so suddenly during the investigation of Mel Sweeten's murder."

"What else could you think?" Mann replied approvingly. "Uncle Manny got to Chief Stillman. I don't know whether he knew I was involved or not. But, as we all know, a person close to Mannheim Goodwillie simply does not get into the newspapers as a murder suspect.

"He pressed down screws and my fiancée and I went to Jamaica for an extended honeymoon."

Mann poured himself another drink and pointed to a framed picture of a pleasant, slightly overweight woman. "My late wife. Did you know her?"

Jackie shook her head. "No."

"Too bad. She was a lovely woman. Only one I ever loved. I had her eighteen days before the accident . . ."

"The *accident*?!" Marcella pounced quickly.

"Save your tape, Ms. Vulture," Mann rasped disgustedly. "It *was* an accident. I'd have given my own life before I let that angel slip away."

Jackie saw in the man's face that he was sincere and felt for him.

"We'd been drinking," Mann explained. "We went up a mountain on bicycles. We get to the top. Took a few pictures. She stepped back too far. Over she went. I was dumbfounded. It was like a Road Runner cartoon. Only it was real. She didn't get back up and dust herself off. She was dead. I buried her. The government was very understanding. Sign a few papers and it was over. So sorry. Dreadful accident. No fuss. No bother. No . . . anything. Not anymore. I came back here, wrote about the experience to my uncle Mannheim. I didn't want anything. Not even his sympathy. It's just that he was all the family I had left. And of course I helped kill my only friend." Mann burst into mawkish sobs.

Jackie pulled out a chair and sat down. Marcella quietly changed her tape.

Mann eventually regained control. "He persisted in regarding this as a touch. Which it wasn't. I told him again and again. He didn't believe me. Had his lawyers tell me I was never to talk to him or write to him again. Can you imagine?"

The others nodded. Knowing his brother, they could well imagine.

"I decided to kill him," Mann said simply. "Not for the money. I don't care about that anymore. I have enough left to drink myself to death." Mann poured himself a drink. "I just wanted to see him suffer for all the suffering he had caused everyone else. My mother lived her whole life for that man. Worked for him since she got out of school. Slaved for him, slept with him. Gave him a child . . ."

Mann saw the other looks and nodded. "Yes, I'm 'Uncle Manny's' illegitimate son. Not that he admitted it. Or that my mother ever pressed him on it. She waited for him until the day she died. Waited for him when he fell for that tramp, the mayor. Waited for him when he went back to his wife. Then it was my turn to wait." Mann indulged himself in a big ugly laugh. "I'm good

with my hands, you see. I fixed this place up, you know?
It had gotten pretty run-down. Bums were living on the
grounds here, tearing boards off the houses to make their
fires. I bought the microwave machine from a man's
action magazine. Set it up in my truck. Parked alongside
the radio station at the right time and pow. Neat, sweet,
everyone thought it had to be one of the people inside
the studio. But it was like the Kennedy assassination,
I set up someone to be the patsy. Unfortunately, Alice
Blue was late."

"You were going to set up Alice Blue?"

"Sure, why not? She's a nut, right? Has access to
the microwave equipment from her husband's hardware
store. Even had a grudge if anyone bothered to check it.
She went to Goodwillie Industries for a defense fund for
her little girlfriend in prison and they turned her down
flat. Threw her out on her ear. It's all right there in
one of her crazy pamphlets. Didn't you even bother to
read the literature?" Mann held up an envelope holding
one of the circulars Jackie remembered seeing the wom-
en stuffing into envelopes when she had visited Alice
Blue's house.

"I figured Uncle Stuart would do what he did," Mann
continued. "Find some poor sap and blame it on them.
If I was lucky no one could trace back any path to me
until I was safely in Jamaica. When the money ran out
or the police started sniffing around, I'd take the same
exit route as my dear Magda."

"But," Jackie supplied. "Just as it seemed you were
going to get away with it, Spike Fitzgerald tried to
blackmail you."

Mann nodded. "He heard the discharge of microwave
energy on his headphones. Looked out the window of
his sound studio and recognized my truck. Just my luck
his wife happened to have a schnauzer I trained years
ago. No more of that now, eh? No, no more dog training
for 'Tom the Dog-Training Man.' What's to become of

my little four-legged friends now? Can anyone answer that? I was their last chance in this world."

"How about getting back to Mr. Fitzgerald?" Marcella piped up.

Mann belched and then nodded. "Deserved it, crooked son of a gun. Got myself interviewed on your program, Ms. Jacobs. Paid the old under-the-table fee. You know about that, right, Marcie? That businessmen pay producers of so-called news shows to do favorable features on them? I got myself booked, brought my little pet Itsy Bitsy, and disposed of my financial partner Spike before I had to give him a dime. Nice thing about a spider. If it doesn't work, who can trace it?" Mann burped again and then turned back to Jackie. "Not like my foolish adventure sending Shag to your mother's house. I denied owning her, but of course that fooled no one."

"What about Arthur Goodwillie?" Jackie asked quietly.

"My half brother?" Mann snorted. "He did away with himself before I could. That's what it was, surely. A suicide. I never met the man. Had nothing against him."

"The will?" Marcella asked.

"Uncle Mannheim's? His money goes into a trust. No, sorry, Ms. Jacobs," Mann sneered. "If I stand to inherit anything at all, it doesn't get any bigger if the other inheritors die. If I was just interested in the money, Arthur was the last person I would have killed. From all accounts, Arthur was a notorious soft touch. I could have wrung hundreds of thousands of dollars from him with my story. No, ladies. I'm not so smart. I'm pretty stupid, in fact. Fat, drunk, and stupid—that's what Uncle Stuart always said about me. And of course he's right, as he is about so many things.

"I'm so stupid I even managed to buy beer that doesn't have any alcohol in it. What with all the dogs and stars and flags on the label, who could tell what it's got inside? So you see . . ." Mann rose to his feet and Jackie and the others saw the sawed-off shotgun in his hand. "I'm not as drunk as it seems." He fired a shot at Carnero, knocking him backward, despite the bulletproof vest he wore.

Jake started to lunge, but Jackie tackled her dog, knowing he didn't have a chance. Mann fired the second barrel over their heads, forcing Marcella to sprawl as well, then ran for the stairs.

Gambling that he would not be able to reload his weapon before Jake could get to him, Jackie released her big dog. "Go!"

As Jackie and Marcella scrambled to their feet, Jackie heard the loud, angry howls of another dog.

"Jake!" Jackie cried out.

She rushed to the back staircase leading to the upstairs room and saw an enormous Great Dane.

Mann stood on the stairs above them, loading his weapon. "Now, I'm going to leave you here to deal with Diablo."

The big dog sat on the third step up, a veritable hydra, barring the exit from Hades.

"I better warn you, Jackie. Diablo eats dogs like yours for snacks. She won't let you up these stairs unless you shoot her. And if you do try to shoot Diablo, you better kill her. Good-bye!"

Carnero staggered out of the kitchen as Mann rushed up the stairs. The big former bodyguard was not hurt beyond a few superficial burns and scratches. He was, however, still a little unsteady from having the wind knocked out of him. Carnero quickly sized up the situation and then raised his pistol as if to shoot Diablo.

"No!" Jackie yelled, pulling down the big lemon ice vendor's arm. "Don't kill her. Not unless we absolutely have to. Let Jake deal with her."

"How's he going to do that?" Marcella asked skeptically.

"Just watch."

Jake did have an idea! As the trio watched, the big

dog worried loose the carpet tacks and pulled hard on the rug runner. The Great Dane gave a surprised whelp as her secure roost suddenly became a steep slide and then, although she pedaled frantically for traction, the guard dog tumbled to the bottom of the stairs.

As Jake streaked up the stairs, Jackie barked instructions. "Marcella! Get a couple of leashes from the kitchen. Carnero, hold her down. Watch her teeth!"

Then, before the Great Dane could fully revive itself, Jackie and her hired muscle managed to get its harness over its mouth and Marcella used two leashes to tie its pairs of legs together.

"Now what?" Marcella gasped when they were finished.

"Call the police!" Jackie ordered. "You've got your story. I've done my bit. Let's let the proper authorities do theirs." Jackie then turned to Carnero. "You drag our friend into one of the other rooms, make sure he's secure, then follow us upstairs. Just make sure when you come up you don't shoot Jake or me."

Carnero shook his head. "No. Let me go first. The man has a loaded gun."

"And I have a loaded dog," Jackie cracked.

"It is not safe!"

Jackie patted the big former bodyguard on the arm, appreciating his genuine concern. "Don't worry. Mann isn't going to shoot us."

Carnero's look was so profoundly skeptical, Jackie continued, "All he wants to do is get away and I'm not going to put us or anyone at risk chasing him. That's the police's job. I'm just going to go up, collect my dog, and go home."

Carnero saw the truth in Jackie's eyes, then reluctantly nodded and let her go while he bent to his task.

Jackie proceeded up the long staircase, quickly coming to the upstairs hall. The long corridor was shrouded in darkness. Jackie didn't know whether the lights simply had not been turned on or whether Mann had doused them irrevocably in his precipitous flight. "Jake!" Jackie called out softly.

After a beat she heard Jake's response, a noise made deep in the old dog's throat.

"Where are you, boy?" Jackie whispered as she carefully felt her way down the hall. "Are you all right?"

Finally, Jackie saw her dog sitting by an open doorway. Too late Jackie realized that he was being held there at gunpoint.

Jackie reached out her hand to pet her loyal companion, when a hand snaked out and grabbed her by the wrist.

"Oh!" Jackie started to cry out but a large hand soon smothered her scream. She felt the cold touch of a metal cylinder against her neck, and heard Tom Mann's voice rasp in her ears.

"Don't move. And tell your dog that too. You know me. I intend to kill myself. Doesn't matter to me if I kill a few more before I go."

Jackie nodded that she would be quiet.

"All right now. No funny stuff," Mann ordered. "I want you to go straight across the hall. Press down the metal lever opening the door, then turn on the light switch to the right. I'm warning you, if I even think you're going to try something, I'll blow a hole in you."

Jackie mumbled something and pointed down at Jake.

"Yeah, he's coming with us," Mann announced. "I'm not letting him run to get help. I've seen Rin Tin Tin too."

The murderer, his reluctant prisoner, and her dog slowly moved into what had been the guest bedroom in the old house. Jackie walked into the small bedroom, bare except for a cot, end table, and ratty bureau, and heard the distressing sound of a dead bolt being slammed home behind her.

"How do you like my room, Jackie?"

"It certainly is Spartan," she commented.

"Yes," Mann replied dryly. "Except for the very rich, like your good friend Stuart Goodwillie, this is how we home owners live. Like janitors, in a basement room, so we can pay our real estate taxes."

Jackie shrugged. "If you couldn't afford the place, why rent it in the first place?"

"Because," Mann replied angrily, "a dog trainer can't operate out of a studio apartment in some tenement, Ms. Walsh. I would have thought even a head-in-the-clouds academic type like yourself could grasp that."

"Do you mind if I sit down?" Jackie asked, her back still to her kidnapper.

"Not scared of what I might do?"

Jackie gave her abductor a tired look. "My feet hurt, Tom. It's been a long day. If you intend to do something to me, my posture's probably not going to stop you."

Mann chuckled grimly. "Right you are. Make yourself comfortable. Like my etchings?"

Jackie glanced at the posters and unframed stills of a dozen radio programs and performances. A couple of the posters, Jackie noted, were actually advertisements for the stage or movie serial versions of the shows, but Mann had taped over that part of the poster, with pieces of construction paper painted with the radio show times and performers.

"Very nice," she commented. "No *I Love a Mystery*?"

"Doesn't exist," Mann said in the high whiny voice that had once reminded Jackie of the great radio comedian Ed Wynn. "Probably a matter of two groups of former cereal manufacturers fighting over the potential profits while the creators and stars of the show starve."

"That's certainly possible," Jackie agreed. "It could also be that there just aren't enough old radio fans to make those sorts of posters profitable."

"You too, eh?" Mann sneered. "Worshiping the almighty profit margin."

"No," Jackie began, but Mann wasn't listening.

"My 'uncle' was like that. Good old 'Bottom Line' Goodwillie. You know, it's not fair. I mean, I don't expect anyone to sympathize with me. Wouldn't do me any good now anyway. But look at those pictures." Mann pointed to a handful of cheaply framed Kodachromes placed on top of the bureau. They depicted a younger, business-suited Mannheim Goodwillie reluctantly horsing around with a young Tommy Mann. "He loved me. I was like a son to him. I was much closer to him than little Arthur—who spent his childhood in private schools in Switzerland. But what did it matter? The fact that I didn't have his name made me a nonperson. A nobody."

"A forgery," Jackie supplied.

"Exactly!" Mann enthused. "I was little Tommy Kruegar Mann, the human forgery. Biologically as much his son as Arthur, but not valued as such. I didn't want his money. Not just his money, anyway. I wanted to have a father."

"I would sympathize with you a lot more, Tom," Jackie said slowly, "if you hadn't killed those people. If you weren't holding Jake and me prisoner."

"What about me?" Mann wailed.

"What about you?"

"Why did all those terrible things have to happen to me?" Mann asked plaintively.

"Why not you?" Jackie replied simply.

Mann was struck dumb for a moment, then someone pounded on the bedroom door.

"Mr. Mann! Open up! This is Lieutenant McGowan of the police."

"No!" Mann backed away reflexively. "Don't come any closer or I'll kill the girl."

"That's not going to help you, Mr. Mann," McGowan replied in a calm voice. "You're not going anywhere and it's just going to be worse for you if you try to hurt anyone else. We know about you and your wife, Mr. Mann. What happened to her is a terrible thing. We have a therapist here who wants to talk with you. If you like, he's willing to become your hostage instead of Ms. Walsh."

Mann started to rub his hand over his face. "I . . . What are you doing to me? You're trying to trick me."

"No, sir," McGowan replied calmly. "I'm a peace officer, Mr. Mann. That's what I try to do, keep the peace. I don't want to see you get hurt. I don't want to see anyone else get hurt. I know you're confused and angry and there's a doctor here who might be able to help you if you'll just give him a chance."

"No!" Mann shouted. "Shut up! Shut up! Leave me alone!" Mann fired his pistol through the door. He then threw open the bedroom window and put one leg outside. "Don't try to follow me," he instructed.

After a moment, Jackie ran for the window. She joined Jake at the sill. Mann had gotten out on the sharply gabled roof. It would have been a difficult traverse for a young, healthy person. And Mann was not young. And Mann was tired, very tired, and, now that his running around had gotten the alcohol into his bloodstream, rather drunk.

As McGowan and Carnero burst in through the door, Jackie saw Mann slip and fall and slide out to the edge and hold on by just his fingertips to the gutter and she felt Jake tense beside her. He wanted to go, but she held him back. Jackie didn't think Jake could get there in time. And when she considered what was at stake here, the life of a murderer against the life of her good and loyal dog, Jackie decided it just wasn't worth the risk.

And so Mann died.

EPILOGUE

Thomas Marland Kruegar Mann's funeral was a quiet affair. Stuart Goodwillie paid for it but did not attend. There were no relatives. No friends. Because the funeral took place on Wednesday, his acquaintances and clients did not come. Nor did the press. They had had their fun and now wanted nothing more to do with him. The only people who attended the funeral of Tom Mann were the same ones who had been with him at the end—Jackie, McGowan, Carnero, and Jake.

When the gravediggers began to fill their shovels, Jackie turned away. McGowan walked with her. She allowed that. He put his arm around her shoulders. She allowed that too.

It was only when he said, "Can I drive you home?" that she balked.

"No, thank you. I'll be all right."

"But Peter's not here," McGowan pointed out. "You'll be alone."

"No, I won't." Jackie smiled sadly, clicking her fingers for her dog as she walked away. "I have Jake."